GOODBYE GIFTS

A Castle Mountain Lodge Romance

ELENA AITKEN

Ink Blot Communications

Also by Elena Aitken

Castle Mountain Lodge

The Springs Series

Chapter One

CARMEN KINCAID TOOK a deep breath and looked over the main lobby of Castle Mountain Lodge. In her role as customer service manager, it was her job to make sure everything was going smoothly, and after a quick scan, everything seemed to be in order. Guests were enjoying their coffee by the fireplace, others were milling about, getting ready to go on outdoor adventures, and at the front desk…Carmen's gaze froze on a customer who was leaning over the desk, looking more than a little agitated.

She pasted on the smile she'd perfected over the years, straightened her blouse and headed over to the front desk to see what was going on.

"Quinn," Carmen said, with a quick smile in the guest's direction. "Is everything okay here?"

Quinn, her best desk clerk, looked up from where he'd been frantically tapping at the keys and said, "Carmen. I'm sorry, but I can't seem to find Mr. Jansen's reservation and he—"

"I'm booked for a family suite," the guest said, his agitation level rising.

"Would it be okay if I took a look?" Carmen smiled at both Mr. Jansen and a relieved-looking Quinn and moved around the desk. After a few quick keystrokes, she looked up from the computer screen, and to the waiting customer. "Mr. Jansen," she said, sweetly. "I have your reservation right here. It looks as if you booked for a family suite, next weekend." She tilted her head in sympathy.

The man, whom a moment ago had been insisting she'd personally screwed up their reservation, looked down, the expression on his face changing in an instant. Despite the fact that he'd been rude to her, Carmen felt for him. His wife and two kids behind him looked exhausted, and clearly, it'd been a long drive up the mountain.

"Next weekend?" He ran his hand through his hair, leaving it sticking up at odd angles. "But we're here now, and the kids...what am I going to do? They'll be so disappointed." He glanced back to his family, before turning his focus on Carmen, pleading with his eyes.

"Let me see what I can do." Carmen gave him a sympathetic smile and turned her attention back to her computer screen. It was a good thing they were into their slow season at Castle Mountain Lodge. Autumn always was a nice reprieve between the busyness of summer and the bustle of the winter ski season. Carmen knew without looking she'd be able to find something for the Jansen family, and after a moment, she proved successful. "I have a room," she whispered, and quickly added, "It's not a suite, but it's the next best thing. It's a family loft, with two beds up, and a comfortable living space below."

"I'll take it."

"Absolutely." Carmen took the man's information, and with a few more keystrokes, she finished the check-in and handed him his welcome packet.

"Thank you so much," he said. "I'm sorry I was a—"

"It's not a problem, Mr. Jansen." She kept her smile in

place, the way she always did. "Honestly. It was my pleasure, and I do hope you and your family enjoy your stay at Castle Mountain Lodge. In your packet, you'll find a list of activities that I'm sure the kids will enjoy."

She watched as they made their way across the large, timber-framed lobby, towards the bank of elevators. There was no doubt in Carmen's mind that Mr. Jansen and his family would find the relaxation and rest they'd come to the Lodge looking for. There was something about the air in the mountains that relaxed even the tensest people.

Carmen set to work adjusting the reservations in the computer, and checking room availability. She hadn't received the phone call confirming her parents' visit yet, but it was coming. For the last three years, since Carmen had gone to work at the Lodge, they made a point to come visit for a long weekend every October. It wasn't necessarily a weekend Carmen looked forward to.

She clicked a few buttons and reserved her parents a nice suite with a view of the ridge. With any luck, they would be preoccupied with their stunning surroundings and less focused on their daughter's lack of husband.

Their weekend visit was bound to be filled with questions about when she was going to give up her "little job" and settle down with a nice boy, or at the very least, go to college where she could meet a nice boy. Just thinking of the way her dad was going to drill her about her future plans, while her mother listed all her friends' young, eligible sons she should meet was enough to fake some sort of deadly illness.

But, Carmen knew better. Nothing would distract her mom and dad from their annual visit. Since she flat-out refused to come back for Christmas, or any other time, it was their duty as good parents to smother their only child with love.

She sighed, and put her head down on the front desk for a moment.

"Working hard, are you?"

The voice jolted her up and Carmen looked directly into the eyes of Trent Harrison, the general manager of the Lodge. Carmen snapped to attention and smoothed her dark hair behind her ears. "Mr. Harrison," she said. "I'm so sorry. I was just...well, I—"

"It's fine." Trent waved away her explanations. "And I told you to call me Trent. Besides, I'm not going to be your boss for much longer."

"That's right," she said. It's not like it was a secret that Trent was leaving to go run a high-scale resort with his brother in a few weeks. What was the secret was who would be filling his position. "You must be excited about your new opportunity," she said. "And you know I refuse to call you by your first name when we're working." Her smile was warm, because outside of work, they were friends, but Carmen liked to keep some sort of professional distance during working hours. So far, it'd served her well in her career. She'd only been at the Lodge for three years and had already worked her way up to customer service manager and with any luck, she'd be a candidate for Trent's job, too.

Trent laughed, his handsome features crinkling in humor. "That's one of the things that's so great about you, Carmen." He ran a hand through his blond, slightly wavy hair. "You're nothing if not professional." He leaned across the desk and lowered his voice. "I hear that you're in the running for my job."

Her stomach flipped, but not because of his proximity. She knew more than one woman who'd love the chance to hook up with Trent, but she'd never been interested in dating anyone she worked with. Or anyone at all, really.

"That's what I'm told," she said. Word had filtered down to her last week that she was one of the candidates for the job.

"Did you also hear that I get to choose my replacement?"

Carmen's heart started beating double time and she blinked hard. "What?"

"Would I lie to you?" She raised her eyebrows and tilted her head, causing him to laugh again. "Okay, I might. And maybe I'm exaggerating a little," he continued. "But I do get a say in the final selection. I'm told that my opinion matters a great deal. And I'm keeping my eye on you." He winked dramatically and she had to laugh.

"I'm sure you are." They'd always been easy friends, not in small part due to her ability to dodge his advances.

He grinned and took a quick look around before changing the subject. "I actually was hoping to ask you something, Carmen. Totally unrelated to work."

Carmen's smile faltered. Trent's affairs at the Lodge were legendary. He didn't date; in fact, in the three years she'd been there, she'd never heard of him dating at all. His affairs, however—that was a different story. So far, she'd managed to keep their relationship professional, probably in no small part due to the fact that she insisted on professionalism with everyone she worked with. Friendly, yes. But there was no way Carmen would ever entertain the thought of dating anyone who worked at the Lodge, particularly someone in a management position. Not if it would risk her career.

"You know I don't—"

"Oh, don't worry. I would never dream of asking you out," he said.

She shot him a look.

"Not that I wouldn't want to," he added quickly. "But I'm not an idiot, Carmen. And only an idiot would bang their head against that wall. I know your policy on dating at work."

Carmen smiled again and nodded. "Okay, then what would you like to ask me?"

"I think you're going to like this." Trent stood up and stretched his shoulders. "My brother is coming to stay at the

Lodge for a few days. Maybe a week, if I can convince him to enjoy himself a little bit. Anyway, I'm going to be busier than I'd like what with wrapping things up around here and all. I was hoping maybe you would show him around a bit."

"Show him around?" Carmen got a sinking feeling in her stomach. And the distinct impression that there was more to his request than he was saying.

"Yes," Trent said. "No one knows the ins and outs of Castle Mountain like you do, and who better than a beautiful woman to keep him company?"

And there it was. The reason Carmen didn't feel good about her boss's request. She tipped her head and assessed him. Despite Trent's reputation as a bit of a womanizer, he'd never been anything but respectful. She must have heard him wrong.

"What about Bo?" she suggested. "He knows the Lodge much better than I do. And as the outdoor activities director, he's the perfect choice."

Trent smiled a little and looked at his feet. "Look, Carmen. I don't usually do this type of thing, but I was kind of thinking Dylan would enjoy the company of a woman."

Carmen pretended to ignore him. "Well, as we know," she said, "where Bo is, Morgan is." They were Castle Mountain Lodge's resident lovebirds, and good friends of Carmen's.

"I was thinking more along the lines of a single woman," Trent said.

As a reflex, Carmen's hand shot out and she smacked his arm. "Trent Harrison," she said. "What type of girl do you think I am?"

Trent's head snapped up and a look of pure mortification took hold on his face. "Oh, God, Carmen. No. Not like that. I just really want him to enjoy himself a little, go out, laugh. That type of thing. I don't mean anything sleazy by it."

She narrowed her eyes and assessed him for a moment. "Really?"

Trent held up two fingers. "I swear."

She shook her head and considered her options. There weren't many. "I don't know, Trent. Like you said, I don't date, and my parents are coming next weekend for their annual visit and with working and—"

"Please, Carmen. I won't take no for an answer. And I'm not looking to marry my brother off or anything. I just really need Dylan to have a little fun before we jump into the fire with the Springs. Besides, he'll probably be gone by the time your folks come."

"Trent, it doesn't feel right and—"

"It'll even be fun for you," he continued. "You work too hard as well, and if you do get the position as general manager, well…"

Her breath caught in her throat and for a minute, Carmen thought she might actually be sick. "What do you mean?" she asked slowly.

"Just that if you do happen to get the position," he paused and raised his eyebrows, "that you'll be very busy for the next little while."

Her instincts told her that wasn't all he meant by his comment. "I'm a long shot for the manager position," she said softly.

Trent leaned in again and lowered his voice before he said, "Remember, I do play a role in the selection of my replacement and it would be an easy decision to choose a candidate who goes above and beyond the call of duty. If you get my drift?"

Carmen swallowed hard. She got his drift all right.

"Think about it," he said.

A group of giggling women came through the main doors

and Trent stood up, adjusting his jacket. He stepped aside and said, "I'll totally owe you, Carmen. We'll talk soon."

She watched him walk through the lobby and disappear down the hall that led to the banquet room.

Did that really just happen? Trent didn't really just tell her she had to take his brother out if she wanted the promotion, did he? Not in so many words, but that was definitely what was implied, right? Unless she'd been reading too much into it. That was probably it; she'd probably just thought he was saying something he wasn't.

Thoughts swirled through her head so quickly, she couldn't focus on just one thing.

She shook her head in a desperate attempt to clear her mind, and focused on the women who were checking in. It was easier to bury herself in work. It always had been.

Dylan Harrison had only been at the Lodge for twenty minutes, but it was all he needed to decide the mountain resort was exactly the type of experience he wanted to recreate at the Springs, the resort he was opening with his brother in only a few more months.

"So, what do you think?" Dylan's brother, Trent, came up behind him and slapped him on the shoulder. "It's pretty magnificent here, isn't it?"

Dylan turned and gave his older brother a brotherly punch to the arm. Trent may be a year older, but Dylan had never missed an opportunity to remind him that he was bigger and stronger. "Hey, man. It's good to see you."

"And you, kid." He raised his eyebrows. "All of you. Getting a little soft, are you?" As soon as he said the words, Trent dodged the punch he'd known was coming. It was part of their routine. Big brother gave little brother a hard time.

Even though it was far from the truth, and they both knew it. Dylan was in excellent shape, a solid wall of muscle; he was definitely not in any danger of getting soft around the middle.

"Hey," Trent said. "Come on. I have so much to show you."

Their greetings complete, they walked together across the lobby and past the check-in desk where Dylan'd left his bags. Trent led him directly to the picture window that framed the back of the room. Despite the fact he'd seen plenty of mountains before, and had spent his fair share of time exploring them, the view took his breath away. There was nothing quite like being there—it was spectacular—and the construction of the Lodge showcased it beautifully.

"It's amazing," Dylan said truthfully. "I can't wait to see the rest of it."

"There's lots of time," Trent said, "since I convinced you to stay for a bit. And really, I can't believe you've never been up here."

Dylan took one more look at the view, and turned to his brother. "Neither can I. But maybe if you'd told me how amazing it was up here, I would've come a bit sooner."

The truth was, Trent had told him how impressive the Lodge was, on more than one occasion. In fact, they were building a lot of their own business venture on how things were done at Castle Mountain, but Dylan had never made the time to visit his brother. Working sixty-hour-weeks, didn't leave much time for anything else, not even family.

Trent gave him a look, and Dylan was sure he would be on the receiving end of a lecture about how hard he worked and how he needed to relax a little and live his life. Instead, Trent smiled and said, "Come with me. There's someone I want you to meet."

Dylan shrugged and followed his brother to the check-in desk where a stunning woman with long dark hair stood behind the desk. She didn't immediately notice them as she was busy tapping on her keyboard, but when Trent cleared his throat, she popped her head up with a well-practiced smile. Dylan was pretty sure he saw that smile wobble when she recognized Trent, but it only lasted a second.

"Trent," the woman said. "What can I help you with?"

"Carmen Kincaid, I want you to meet my little brother, Dylan."

Dylan extended his hand and locked eyes with the most stunning eyes he'd ever seen. They reminded him of a glacier-fed mountain lake he'd hiked to once, so cool and green, and beautifully compelling. "Carmen," he said, enjoying the way her name felt on his tongue. "It's nice to meet you."

Her eyes flicked shut for a split second before she put her hand in his and he gently squeezed it. He had to resist the ridiculous urge to kiss it. There was something very compelling about the dark-haired beauty. He'd have to settle for a handshake.

"Likewise," she said. "Welcome to Castle Mountain Lodge. Trent has only told me a little bit about you. But he did mention you'd never been here before. I hope you enjoy your stay."

There was something about her eyes that Dylan could not look away from. "I'm sure I will," he said. "So far I like everything I've seen."

Dylan wished he could think of something wittier to say, but words totally eluded him. He held her gaze, and to his surprise and distinct pleasure, she didn't look away. He didn't let go of her hand right away, enjoying the warmth and weight of it in his own. It was only when Trent cleared his throat that Dylan remembered his manners and with an apologetic smile, he released her.

"Carmen is the customer service manager here," Trent said. "She's a huge asset to the Castle Mountain Lodge team, and she's actually being considered to fill my position after I'm gone."

Dylan thought he saw Carmen blanch, but whatever emotions had passed over her face were gone, replaced by a warm smile she aimed in Trent's direction. Dylan had the sudden and insane urge to pull her back so she was facing him with that smile. Their whole life, Trent always got the girl, while Dylan played the role of the wingman. Not that Trent kept the girl very long. He wasn't known for his long-term relationships. And it wasn't that his older brother was better looking than Dylan either, he knew that. He also knew it was easier to play the sidekick role, because he didn't have time for women in his life anyway. And even if he did, women seemed to pick up his vibe of indifference, and kept their distance.

"Well, congratulations," Dylan managed to say. "That sounds like a great opportunity."

"Thank you."

The three of them stood awkwardly for a few moments before Trent said, "Carmen really has a reputation of going above and beyond for the Lodge, don't you, Carmen?"

She narrowed her eyes at Trent, and Dylan had the distinct impression he was in the middle of a private issue.

"Well," Dylan said uncertainty. "That's great. In fact, that sounds like exactly the type of person we need at the Springs. Any chance we can convince you to move?" He was joking, but both Trent and Carmen looked taken aback, so he added, "Or at the very least, maybe you can give me some tips about what to look for?"

Trent smacked him on the arm. "That's a great idea, brother. Isn't it, Carmen?"

They both looked towards Carmen. Dylan had just been making small talk, but now that the invitation was out there, he did think it was a great idea. Any excuse to spend more time with her.

"In fact," Trent said. "Maybe you could show him around the Lodge a little bit, too."

He saw the uncertainty cross her face, and Dylan held his breath that she'd say yes. Suddenly, he wanted nothing more than to spend some time with the beautiful woman in front of him, and he couldn't remember the last time he'd felt like that about any woman.

She looked between the brothers, a question in her eyes. "Actually," Carmen said after what seemed like a very long time. "Trent beat me to it, but I was going to ask you if you'd be interested in meeting me for a drink later so I could point out a few of the finer points of the Lodge. What do you think?"

What did he think? He thought it'd been awhile since he'd been asked on a date, and the very last thing he needed while he was at the Lodge was the distraction of a woman, but at that moment he couldn't think of anything he'd like more.

"We do have a lot of business to take care of while I'm here," Dylan said. He couldn't even believe the words that came out of his mouth. He should be jumping at her invitation, but old habits die hard. And work came first.

"I'm sure you can sneak away at some point, Dyl," Trent said. "We have the meeting with the Braxtons later, but maybe after that?"

Dylan nodded, and locked eyes with Carmen. That cinched it. "Sounds great," he said. "It would be nice to hear about the inner workings of a resort like this from someone besides my brother."

She smiled, and ducked her head a little, causing a strand to fall over her eye. Dylan stuffed his hands in his pockets to keep from reaching out and tucking it behind her ear.

"So later, then?" she said.

"Sounds good."

Trent and Dylan left Carmen alone to finish her shift, and

more importantly to them, so they could get ready for the first of what were going to be very important meetings.

Trent showed Dylan the meeting rooms where they'd be conducting the majority of their business, including a makeshift office area for Dylan.

"I knew you'd want your own space, little brother." Trent waved his arm around the boardroom with a printer and a few office supplies set up on one end. "It's not much, but it's better than working out of your room. Plus here, you have a view."

And what a view it was. Dylan turned and stared out the window at the majestic mountains. Even with all the time he'd been spending in Cedar Springs, the small town where the Springs resort would be based, Dylan hadn't had much time to actually enjoy the mountains and all they had to offer. Even just staring at them seemed to be enough to bring down his blood pressure and give him a moment to relax.

All Dylan had been doing lately was working. While Trent had hung on to his full-time job, Dylan had focused solely on getting the construction of the Springs resort going, and pulling together the financing they'd need to complete the project on time. Together, the brothers were building one of the biggest resorts in the Rocky Mountains, based around a little known naturally occurring hot spring that up until recently had been a local secret.

He was so lost in the view, Dylan failed to keep up with Trent's chatter about their impending meeting. It took him a moment, but Dylan focused on the task at hand.

"Everything's ready on my end," Dylan said. "We still have an hour or so?"

"About that." Trent looked at his wristwatch. "I need to run and take care of a few things. But you should find everything you need in the room next door. The Braxtons will be here in just under an hour and we can get started. If you need anything else, don't hesitate to give the front desk a call.

Carmen will take care of anything you need." Trent wiggled his eyebrows and if he'd been standing any closer, Dylan would have punched him. "She's hot, right?"

Of course he agreed, but he wasn't going to give his brother that satisfaction. Instead, he shrugged.

"You can't fool me, little brother." Trent laughed. "She's a hottie and I know you think so. I'd have to disown you if you didn't. And lucky you, she seems interested. Not that I know why." He rolled his eyes. "But maybe you can have a little fun while you're here? You work too hard."

"I'm fine," Dylan said. "Besides, I could say the same for you."

"Maybe," Trent said. "But you're the one going for drinks with Carmen. Not me."

Before he could reply, Trent left to take care of his business, and Dylan was left alone. He knew he should be using every moment he had to prepare things for the meeting, but he couldn't keep his mind off the dark-haired beauty with the intense eyes, and the promise of spending more time with her.

Chapter Two

SHE HAD a busy day ahead of her, and definitely didn't have time to think about Trent, or more specifically, his brother, Dylan. But Carmen couldn't seem to do much of anything else since running into them in the lobby.

Dylan was insanely good-looking with his dark hair and dark eyes. But there was more to him than just his looks. She'd felt it the moment she'd locked eyes with him. What was that saying, still waters run deep? That's what it was. He didn't say much, but she could tell there was a lot going on in his head. Maybe she'd actually have a chance to see what was going on with him, since they'd be going out for a drink later.

Why had she asked him out? The question ran through her head for the dozenth time even though she knew exactly why. He was incredibly gorgeous and there'd been no doubt that there was a spark between them. If anyone asked, that's what she'd say. That's why she broke her no-dating rule. It had nothing to do with what Trent said earlier or may or may not have been implied. Nothing to do with helping her get the job of her career. No. She shook her head.

Carmen took a deep breath and straightened her shirt in an effort to refocus on her work. She stared at the computer screen, but didn't see any of the names or reservation details. She needed to think about something else. There was no point in making herself crazy over something she couldn't change after the fact. She might as well just enjoy her drinks with Dylan. That's all it was. Nothing more.

She was still standing behind the desk when the arrival of a young couple provided the perfect distraction. "Hello," she said, slipping easily into her role, "and welcome to Castle Mountain Lodge. My name is Carmen. How can I help you today?"

"We're checking in," the man said.

"He surprised me with this trip for our one-year anniversary," his wife said. "Isn't he the sweetest?"

Carmen smiled genuinely. "That's very sweet." She felt a twinge of jealousy as she processed the check-in. The couple in front of her was roughly the same age as she was, and they'd found happiness. She wondered what the woman did for a living. Had she given up her future for her husband? It was a ridiculous thought and one Carmen knew she had no business in having, but she couldn't help it.

For a crazy moment, she considered asking the woman if it was worth it, but common sense prevailed and she handed over their welcome package and sent them on their way.

When the couple was out of sight, she dropped her head to the desk and silently reprimanded herself.

"Are you okay?"

The voice shocked her back to her senses, and Carmen jolted up right, looking directly into Dylan Harrison's eyes.

Perfect.

"Mr. Harrison," she said, stumbling over his name. "How can I help you this afternoon? I hope everything is okay. If there's anything I can—"

"It's fine." He held up his hand and smiled. It wasn't Trent's lady-killer smile, but it sent a shock through her and she blushed. "I wasn't coming to complain," he said.

Carmen forced herself to relax. She took a breath and said, "Well, I'm glad to hear that. What can I help you with then?"

A ridiculous part of her hoped he wasn't coming to cancel on their date, or whatever it was. Even though that might be the best solution to the situation she'd put herself into. Trent couldn't hold it against her if she'd tried to take Dylan out and he'd canceled. Not that it would help her with her currently skewed sense of right and wrong. She wasn't thinking clearly.

Dylan crossed his arms, and leaned on the desk. "It's not a big deal, really," he said, his eyes never leaving hers. "But I have a meeting starting in twenty minutes in the Spruce Room, and Trent said there'd be a projector for me to use."

She nodded. "He did mention that." Carmen turned to her computer and started tapping on the keyboard. "Yes," she said. "He reserved the Spruce Room, a screen, and coffee service. But there's no projector on the order."

"Really? Leave it to Trent to forget the details." Dylan sighed, but he didn't look angry. "I'm sorry." He stood and shrugged apologetically. "Is there any way we can get one on such short notice?"

"Of course, Mr. Harrison. I'll figure it out right away." She reached for the phone. "I'm so sorry for the inconvenience."

"It's no trouble," Dylan said. "It wasn't your fault. And please, call me Dylan." His lips curled up into a smile again, and for a second, Carmen lost focus.

"Sorry, it's habit."

"No problem." He tapped his hand on the desk and turned to leave.

It wasn't until he'd disappeared down the hall that she shook herself out of the trance she was in and punched in the number for Erin, who was in charge of managing the boardrooms and meeting rooms. She had a job to do and it wasn't going to get done if she didn't stop behaving like a silly school girl. She'd never let a man affect her like that before, and she wasn't about to start now. Especially with a man who happened to be Trent Harrison's brother and that she happened to invite out for a date only to further her career. It was skeevy. It was awful, and totally not like her. The last thing she needed was to develop actual feelings for him.

Erin picked up the extension, and Carmen immediately barked into the phone. "I need a projector."

"Pardon me?"

Carmen caught herself. It wasn't like her to snap at the other employees. She prided herself on handling even the toughest situations with grace. She took a breath and tried again. "I'm sorry. It's not your fault, but I need to know if we have a projector available for a guest meeting. It was left off the order and he has a presentation in less than twenty minutes."

"We should have," Erin said. "Just give me a…yes. I have one. I can—"

"No," Carmen interrupted. "I'll do it." She scanned the lobby. It was slow, and as the customer service manager, she really should take care of these issues herself. At least, that's what she told herself.

"Carmen, you really don't have to—"

"It's fine," she said. "I'll be right there to pick it up. Mr. Harrison is an important guest. I want to see to this problem myself."

And, she thought. Carmen quickly dismissed the thought. No. She was just trying to do her job to the best of her ability. That was it. There was nothing more to it.

She hung up the phone and with a quick word to Joe, who was manning the other check-in computer, she took off for the events office.

Even as she walked down the corridor, she knew there was more to her quest to keep Dylan Harrison a satisfied guest of the Lodge. How could there not be? Ever since he'd looked at her, she hadn't been able to get him out of her head. The whole thing was ridiculous and if she could just see him again, in a professional capacity, she'd certainly be able to diffuse whatever it was that was going on in her head.

"Carmen, I'm so sorry that there was a mix-up," Erin said as soon as she stepped into the room. The woman handed the projector case to Carmen. "It wasn't on the list and—"

"Don't worry. It wasn't your fault. I'll take care of it."

She immediately spun on her heel and before Erin could trip over herself with any more apologies that weren't necessary, she headed out the room and down the hall towards the conference rooms.

There was only ten minutes before the meeting started when Carmen walked in the room. She expected to find Dylan buzzing around, stressed because of his lack of equipment, and generally behaving as she would if things weren't going according to plan and she had an important meeting. Instead, she found him lounging in one of the chairs, his leg crossed at the knee, flipping through a sheaf of papers.

She stopped in the doorway before announcing herself. It was ridiculous. More than ridiculous, but he looked so at ease. So comfortable and calm that she didn't want to disturb him. Of course, she must have moved, or made a noise, or maybe he just sensed her, but he spun around easily in his chair. When he saw her, his face split into a smile.

"Carmen," he said as he stood and crossed the room towards her. "You didn't have to come." He took the projector from her, but locked eyes with her for a moment. "But I'm glad you did."

Her mind spun with what that comment was supposed to

mean. There was no way it could mean that he was glad to see her; he'd just seen her at the front desk.

"I really need this projector." Dylan moved over to the boardroom table and started unpacking the equipment. "The investors will be here any minute, and without it, my whole presentation would be useless." He looked up and met her eyes again. "You're a real lifesaver, Carmen. Thanks."

Of course. He's just happy to get the equipment. She forced the smile that suddenly felt hard to hold. "Just doing my job," she said. "Good luck with your presentation, Dylan."

She turned to leave. The disappointment at his lack of response rushed through her, followed by confusion, which was ridiculous. He was a means to an end for her. Even if it was underhanded, and beneath her to accept Trent's offer, she'd done it. And now she had to live with it. It would be a whole lot easier if she stopped whatever feelings she was having for Dylan altogether.

"Carmen?"

Automatically, she turned to look at him, a thrill slicing through her at the sound of her name on his lips.

"You do your job really well," he said. "I'll see you later?"

"Of course." She sucked in her bottom lip and nodded her head.

Before he could say anything else that concreted exactly how ridiculous Carmen's feelings for him were becoming, she left. Carmen got all the way down the hall before she stopped and leaned up against the wall, tipped her head up to the ceiling and closed her eyes.

No. This can't happen. None of this can happen, she told herself, forcing her thoughts to slow.

She took a deep breath and exhaled loudly.

She needed to tell Trent that whatever he was playing at, it was over. She wouldn't sacrifice her morals just to get a leg up with the job. She couldn't do it. Especially with someone like

Dylan. She needed space from him, not closeness, not if she was going to escape unscathed. It was probably for the best anyway. No. It was definitely for the best. She opened her eyes and pushed off the wall, running smack into a solid, very male chest.

"Carmen."

"Trent?"

His hands squeezed her upper arms, steadying her.

"Are you okay? I'm sorry," he said. "I didn't see you there and I wasn't really expecting you to—"

"I'm fine." She wiggled out of his grasp and tugged on her blouse to straighten it. "Actually, I was going to come and find you because, I just can't—"

"I was hoping to see you, too." He eyed her with suspicion, but there was no point in getting into anything with him. "I'm really happy you decided to take me up on my offer with Dylan. I know the two of you will have a great time together and—"

"No." She shook her head. "I can't do it, Trent."

He tipped his head and smirked. "Why? Is it his looks? I know he's not as handsome as his big brother, but I didn't think—"

"Stop it. That's not it. I just don't feel right about it." She took a step backwards, needing distance. "I…I just…"

"You want the job, don't you?" His straightforwardness grabbed her attention. "I'm sorry, I didn't mean that." He took a deep breath and looked around a little uncomfortably. "Look, Carmen. Let me be straight with you."

She stared at him, waiting for more.

"I don't make a practice of abusing my position with the staff, but I really need a little help here. My little brother refuses to take any time off and I'm worried about him."

Carmen nodded. Despite how he'd approached it, he did seem to genuinely mean what he was saying. The look of concern in his eyes was real and Trent really wasn't a bad guy. "I'm listening."

"I'm just trying to be a good brother. And I'd really appreciate it, okay? It's not like anyone's going to get hurt and if you can do me this little favor, I promise to put in a good word with management. It's win-win, really. Plus, it's not like he's a bad guy. A bit of a workaholic maybe, but he's a good guy and he's not going to take advantage of you or anything. Who knows, maybe you'll actually enjoy yourself."

That's what she was afraid of, but she didn't say so.

She stared at Trent, looking for any hint of insincerity. Something that would tell her he was being a jerk and totally stepping out of line. But really, he did just seem to be a concerned brother. It would be like doing a favor for a friend; she just wouldn't think of the added bonus there might be at the end of it. Slowly, Carmen nodded. "Okay," she said. "I'll do it."

"Thanks, Carmen. I owe you. And like I said, maybe you'll actually have fun with him."

She bit her lip and turned away. Because that's exactly what she was afraid of. Before he could say anything else, Carmen scurried down the hall and back to the front desk. With any luck, she'd be able to immerse herself in work and forget about everything else, because whatever attraction, or whatever it was that she was feeling for Dylan, it wasn't going to happen. She wouldn't let it.

The phone rang, and she looked around for her front desk staff, who didn't seem to be anywhere in sight. With a sigh, she snatched it up on the second ring. "Castle Mountain Lodge. It's a beautiful day in the Rockies. My name is Carmen, how can I help you?"

"It's so cute how you answer the phone, Carmen." Her mother's voice came over the line. "I can just picture you at your little desk every time you say that."

Carmen winced at her mom's dismissive tone. She knew she wasn't trying to be that way; it was just the way her mom was. If she wasn't baking cookies for a husband and child in some sunny kitchen somewhere, she wasn't living up to her full potential, according to her mom.

"Well, I am at the front desk, Mom," she said. "And I have quite a bit of work to do, so can we talk later?"

"Oh, of course you do, dear," her mother said. "But this will just take a minute. I was just calling to let you know that your dad and I can't come up for Thanksgiving."

Despite the fact that they drove her crazy and were completely condescending about her career choices, Carmen felt the sting of disappointment.

"Why not? I thought you were looking forward to it. Is everything okay?"

"Yes, yes." Carmen could picture her fluttering around and waving her hand as if she could see it through the phone. "But we've been invited to a big potluck at the club and these things are always so much fun," she said. "I'm going to make my potato casserole. You know, the one with the hash browns and the sour cream? But you can't tell anyone it uses hash browns. I like people to think I chop all those potatoes myself, you know?"

"Yes, Mom. I know." Carmen rolled her eyes. "But why is the club having a potluck on Thanksgiving? Aren't people with their families?"

"We'll do it on the Saturday, of course. That leaves lots of time for turkey on the Sunday and Monday." She spoke as if it'd been obvious and Carmen hadn't been paying attention to a word she said. "But it's hardly worth us coming out for a day, is it?"

"No, Mom." Carmen rubbed her temple and took a deep breath. "I suppose it's not."

"That's what we thought. So we'll see you this weekend, then."

"Okay, Mom, that's—wait. What?"

"This weekend," her mom repeated. "It makes perfect sense for us to come up this weekend. We don't have plans and you're always saying how it's your slow season at your little hotel, so why not."

She let the comment about the little hotel slide and focused on the real problem. "But, this weekend?"

"Is it a problem?"

Carmen knew it was a loaded question. Of course it was a problem. She needed time to psychologically prepare for a visit from her parents. Plus, at Thanksgiving, she could usually find small issues to busy herself with so she didn't need to spend too much time with them. But if they came in two days…and there was the small matter of Dylan Harrison and her promise to spend time with him. She shook her head. No. Dylan couldn't impact her decision. Why should he? There was only one way to answer her mother.

"Of course it's not a problem, Mom," she lied, forcing herself to smile. "I can't wait to see you guys."

"Oh good. We'll be there before you know it."

That was exactly what she was afraid of.

"A real lifesaver?" Dylan spoke to the empty room. "Did I really just say that to her?" He slammed his palm down on the table and shook his head.

Ever since Carmen had left the room, he'd been beating himself up over his stupid choice of words. Could he be any lamer? He was an absolute moron in the female department. He was ridiculously out of practice talking to a woman.

"You do your job really well." He mimicked the words. "I'm seriously an idiot."

"Yes you are, brother. But I'll defend you if anyone says it."

Dylan turned around at the sound of Trent's voice.

"Why are you an idiot today?"

The last thing Dylan wanted to do was confide his women troubles to Trent. Not that they were troubles so much as a complete inability to say anything intelligent to a woman he found remotely attractive. And he did find Carmen attractive. More than he wanted to admit. And there was no way he'd be admitting it to Trent, anyway. There was no point.

"Because we didn't have the projector for the meeting," Dylan lied. "Carmen just rushed it down here for me."

Trent raised an eyebrow. "Well, I hope you didn't give her a hard time. She looked a little frazzled to me."

Frazzled? Hopefully not because of anything he'd said or done. Or maybe, not said. Dylan dismissed the thought and shook his head. "Of course I didn't. She's great. Besides, it wasn't her fault you forgot to put the projector on the order."

"I did no such…oh, yeah. I probably did," Trent admitted. "I have a million freakin' things going on and if I forget one or two things, you're just going to have to deal. I can't wait to be done here. I can't keep anything straight anymore."

Dylan gave his brother a quick once-over. "You're sure you're okay with leaving the Lodge? I know how much you like it up here and nothing's guaranteed with the Springs. If it doesn't work out, I don't know what we're going to—"

"It's going to work out," Trent said quickly. "Besides, there's no reward without a little risk, right? Isn't that what Dad used to say?"

"Dad used to say a lot of things," Dylan mumbled.

Ignoring him, Trent walked around the table and opened his briefcase. He pulled out a stack of shiny folders. "I had these made up," he said and handed one to Dylan. "I like them. What do you think?"

Dylan took the glossy folder in his hands and examined it. On the front there was a photograph of mountains, not unlike the ones out the window. "The Springs" was in large bold script across the picture. It was classy and understated, just the way the brothers pictured their resort to be. He flipped it open and scanned the information inside.

"I included all the financial projections, as well as the floor plan and progress pictures of the hotel," Trent said, explaining the pages Dylan was looking at. "I know the investors are mostly interested in the bottom line," he continued. "But I thought it was important for them to see exactly what we're hoping to accomplish with this development."

"I agree." Dylan nodded and closed the folder. "It's great, Trent. And in my presentation, I have the latest images from the job site and a few shots of the town and lake. The resort is going to be the whole package and more than just a place to go for healing and spa treatments. I want to offer the outdoor experience, as well. I like what you do here at the Lodge. I think we should be able to incorporate some of that into our plans as well."

Trent walked around the table, setting a folder in each place. "I agree one hundred percent, brother. And I think the Braxtons will too."

Dylan hoped he was right. They needed the Braxton family to get on board with their vision, which is why they'd brought them all the way to Castle Mountain Lodge. The Braxtons ran a successful chain of resorts and hotels in the Eastern states, but it was rumored they were looking for an expansion plan, and what better investment than a thermal hot springs spa in the Canadian Rockies? Dylan and Trent had used their own substantial savings, not to mention bank loans and other investors, to get them as far as they had in their development.

But in order to take it to the next level and be on track to open their exclusive resort in time for the busy summer tourist season, they were going to need the backing of the Braxtons.

"Don't worry, Dylan. We've got this," Trent said. He straightened his tie, smoothed his suit and gave Dylan a confident smile. "Oh, and if we can convince them to stay at the Lodge tonight, I'll handle the wining and dining."

"Don't you mean, we both will?"

"You're meeting Carmen for a drink, remember?" Trent wiggled his eyebrows and Dylan shot him a look. "Okay fine," Trent said with a laugh. "I know it's not like that. But I do need you to relax. You deserve it. Go have some fun. I can handle the Braxtons."

Dylan had most definitely not forgotten about his date with Carmen, if he could even call it that. Besides, he had responsibilities to Trent and their project. "I'll meet her later," he said. "First we need to take care of this deal. Drinks can wait."

Trent narrowed his eyes. "You're really going to blow off a date with Carmen?"

"That's not what I'm doing," Dylan answered too quickly. He took a breath and continued, "But this is important."

"I got this, Dyl. Trust me." Trent flashed him a toothy grin. "Besides, maybe you can talk to her about an idea I had."

"What's that?"

Trent paused for a moment before he said, "I know you were kidding earlier, but I've been thinking about what you said about Carmen being perfect to come work for the Springs."

"I thought you said she was up for the general manager position here?" Dylan narrowed his eyes and tried to figure out what his brother was up to. He couldn't be sure, but he knew there was something more going on that Trent wasn't saying. "Why would she want to give that up to come work for an unknown resort?"

Trent shrugged. "Maybe just get a feel for it," he said. "I

mean, I wouldn't bring it up right away, but maybe you can plant the seed of change with her. You're good at that type of thing," he continued. "Make it seem like it's her idea. That way if she doesn't get the job here, she'll have options. And she really is good at her job."

Trent wouldn't meet his eyes, furthering Dylan's suspicions that he was up to something. But before he could push the issue any further, there was a knock on the door and Sam Braxton, the patriarch of the family, followed by his son, Les, entered the room, and there was no more room for discussion.

***

Dylan could hardly keep his mind on the important meeting taking place around him. He should have been focused on listening and answering the questions that could make or break the Springs resort, but instead he found his mind constantly drifting to Carmen and the idea of spending some time with her. Maybe he could even repair some of the damage he'd done with his stupid comments earlier.

As the meeting started to wrap up, Dylan glanced at his watch and jumped on the opportunity to seal the deal for the evening. He stood and shook Sam Braxton's hand.

"Thank you so much for coming all the way up to the Lodge," Dylan said. "I do hope you see now what we're hoping to accomplish with the Springs in creating a similar type of atmosphere. Although, as we said, the Springs will definitely have a spa feel, and be primarily a place of relaxation, escape, and healing."

"Of course," Sam Braxton said. "You both did an excellent job conveying that, and my son and I have a lot to consider."

"I do hope you'll be taking us up on our invitation to stay at the Lodge tonight and enjoy everything Castle Mountain has to offer," Dylan said. "Trent will be happy to show you around some of the finer points of the Lodge." Dylan avoided making eye contact with Trent and continued, "No one knows the Lodge better than he does."

"Is that right?" Sam looked to Trent and then to his son. "I think we did plan on staying," he said. "At least for one night. Isn't that right, son?"

"Might as well," Les said. "We've come all this way. It would be a pity not to enjoy it."

"Excellent," Dylan said. "And I wish I could join you, but I have a prior engagement." He pushed back his chair and stood.

"That's a shame," Sam Braxton said. "I was looking forward to asking you a few more questions regarding the financials."

Dylan hesitated, his desire to be with Carmen warring with his commitment to the project.

"Perhaps we can set something up for lunch tomorrow," Trent jumped in. "Unfortunately, Dylan has an important meeting tonight regarding staffing for the Springs." Dylan shot Trent a look, but his brother continued speaking. "We're already starting to put the key staff members in place, and I'm sure you'd agree, proper staffing is crucial to the success of the venture."

Sam nodded his head. "Staff is important," he agreed. "I'd be happy to meet you for lunch tomorrow."

"It's settled, then," Trent said.

Dylan nodded and shook the man's hand. "Well, I'll leave you in my brother's very capable hands," he said. "Thank you, gentlemen. It was a pleasure."

Dylan slipped from the room and all but ran down the hall to the elevator. He took another quick look at his watch. Perfect. He had enough time to go back to his room, change into something that wasn't a suit, and meet Carmen at the Grill.

He ignored the little voice in his head that was telling him he didn't have time for women. Dylan was a businessman, married to his job; there was no room for anything, or anyone else in his life. That was the way it'd always been and with the Springs resort set to open in less than a year, he didn't see that changing anytime soon. But there was something about Carmen that made him forget all of that. He had to know more about her, even if it didn't make any sense at all.

Chapter Three

ALL CARMEN HAD BEEN able to think about all afternoon was meeting Dylan for a drink. The moment her shift was over, she grabbed her purse and ducked out the side door to head back to the employee residence and change into something that wasn't her uniform. She took her time walking through the wooded path, enjoying the quiet of the crisp fall evening, forcing herself to calm down and reminding herself that she wasn't meeting Dylan as a date. She was only going out with him as a favor to Trent. A favor that could very well lead to a promotion.

Her roommate and friend, Astrid, was just leaving the apartment when Carmen arrived.

"Are you coming to the bonfire tonight?" Astrid asked her. "It's probably going to be the last one before it snows and then we'll be stuck inside. You have to come."

Astrid knew as well as she did that Carmen rarely partied with the rest of the staff, but it didn't stop her friend from trying.

"Sorry," Carmen said. She continued to talk to Astrid,

who'd followed her into her room, while she changed. "I actually have plans tonight."

"You do not." Astrid dropped to the bed.

Carmen spun to look at her friend. With her long braids pulled back in a bandanna and an oversized cable knit sweater worn over ripped jeans, she looked every bit the woodsy hippy throwback she was. And despite their differences, Carmen loved her. Astrid had moved in with her almost a year ago, when Morgan, a mutual friend of theirs, moved in with the outdoor activities director, Bo. Carmen made a mental note to talk to Bo about finding something for her parents to do next week.

"I do," Carmen said, focusing on the conversation. She winked at Astrid and pulled a soft sweater over her head.

"Like a date?" Astrid had sat up and was listening with rapt attention. Carmen going on a date was big news. "Please tell me it's a date. Or even just a fling. You know how I feel about boyfriends. But boys…they're all right."

Carmen laughed. "It's hardly a date," she said. "I'm just taking Trent's brother, Dylan, out for a drink to show him the Lodge. He's here for a few days and—"

"Wait." Astrid jumped up. "You're telling me that you're going out with Trent Harrison's brother? That's juicy."

"It's not." Carmen wiggled into a worn pair of jeans and turned to look at herself in the mirror. "It's nothing. Just a drink."

Astrid let out a low whistle. "Whatever you say. But by the way you're getting ready I'd say it's a bit more than that."

Carmen froze before putting on lip gloss. She capped the tube and made a point of putting it back on the dresser. "It's nothing," she repeated and walked out of the room.

Astrid was hot on her heels.

"Besides," Carmen added. "Weren't you telling me that I needed to have more fun?"

Astrid laughed and together they walked out the door. "I did say that, you're right. Go have fun." They reached the fork in the path—one way led to the bonfire, the other direction, back to the Lodge. The two friends parted ways, and Astrid called back to Carmen, "And don't do anything I wouldn't do."

Carmen laughed and shook her head. That didn't leave a lot of options, she thought with a smile.

She still had time, so she took the long way through her favorite trail back to the Lodge. So late in the season there wasn't much of a risk of bears, and although she probably should be more concerned with cougars, Carmen had always thought the risk was worth the reward. There was nothing better than a quiet evening walking through the trees, listening to the sound of the owls calling in the distance, it was Carmen's little bit of therapy and if all it took to keep her grounded, was being alone in the mountains at night, even for a few minutes, she'd take it.

She was enjoying her walk, and too soon she arrived at the main lodge. It's not that she wasn't looking forward to spending time with Dylan; she was. And under any other circumstance, she'd probably be really excited about it. But with Trent's words looming over her, she couldn't shake the heavy feeling that clouded over her.

When Carmen walked into the Grill, she didn't immediately see Dylan, and waving off the hostess's help, she scanned the room herself.

"Carmen."

She turned in the direction of the voice and saw Dylan standing and waving his arm in her direction.

A heat filled her, and traveled through her body the way it had earlier when she'd seen him. She smiled and walked towards him. Regardless of why she was there, she made the split-second decision to enjoy herself, and that wasn't likely to be very difficult.

"Hi, Dylan," she said as she approached his table. He towered over her, and even dressed in a more relaxed sweater and jeans, he was still an imposing presence. A thrill ran through her, and she flinched, hoping he hadn't noticed. "I hope your presentation went well and it wasn't too thrown off by the lack of the projector. I really am sorry."

"Please," he said and waved her protests away. "It wasn't your fault at all. And if it wasn't for you, I don't know what I would have done." He smiled and Carmen noticed a dimple in his left cheek that she hadn't seen before. "I should be thanking you," he said. "And I plan to. I'm glad we could make this work." Dylan held out his hand and gestured to the empty seat across from him.

"Me too," she said as she slipped into the seat across from him and waited for him to sit as well. He gestured to the waitress, who came over and they placed their drink orders. He surprised her by ordering a beer.

"I'm usually a whisky man," he said. "But there's something about being out in the mountains—it brings out my inner mountain man." He grinned and Carmen laughed. She found herself relaxing in his presence. There was something about Dylan that was easy and low pressure, and despite the flutter in her stomach every time he looked at her, or maybe because of it, Carmen couldn't help but feel that her evening might turn out all right after all.

"How did your meeting go today?" She knew it was a lame question, but for lack of anything better to say, it would have to do.

Dylan didn't seem to think it was lame, though, and his face lit up as he said, "It actually went really well. I think we're going to be able to secure the Braxtons and everything will stay on track with the project dates, which is great because after coming up to the Lodge, I'm more excited than ever. It's really great of you to offer to show me a few things. There's so much more I want to know about how things are done up here."

Carmen sat back and smiled. "I'm glad it went well," she said. "And really, I'm happy to help out."

He surprised her by saying, "I hope there might be more to it than just helping."

"Pardon?" She was pretty sure she knew what he meant, but she really needed him to say it.

"I like you, Carmen." Dylan reached across the table and took her hand. Out of habit, she wanted to pull it back and tuck it away in her lap, but there was something comforting about Dylan's touch and she found herself enjoying it. "And I know my big brother can be kind of pushy sometimes." Carmen smirked. "Okay, he can be a lot pushy," Dylan added. "So I hope you didn't feel pressured in meeting me tonight."

Carmen forced the smile to stay in place. If he only knew the half of it, she thought. Dylan didn't need to know that his brother had more or less strong-armed her into meeting him. He especially didn't need to know that, since she would have been happy to go out with Dylan all on her own.

"I like you, too," she surprised herself by saying. The words were immediately followed by a blush. She yanked her hand back and covered her face. "I can't believe I said that."

Not only was she breaking every rule she'd ever made for herself about her career and climbing the ladder honestly, Carmen was also acting like a complete lovesick idiot in front of the one man she'd actually found herself attracted to. The whole situation was more than just a little messed up.

She looked up into his grinning face. "I'm sorry," she said.

"Oh, don't be." Dylan tried not to laugh. "It's nice to know I'm not the only one lacking in dating etiquette," he said. "That is what this is, right?"

Carmen leaned back in her chair and fidgeted with the water glass in front of her. "I thought it was more of a 'get together' thing," she teased. "In fact, you should probably know that I don't date. Ever."

She didn't miss the flicker in his dark eyes before he looked away. Was it disappointment? Defeat? Carmen wanted to sink into the floor and disappear. She racked her brain for something to say. Anything to get him to look at her again with those amazingly deep eyes that captivated her.

"Which isn't to say—"

"That's okay, I don't—"

They spoke at the same time. He smiled and held out his hand to her, urging Carmen to continue. "Ladies first."

She smoothed her hair back from her face, lifting it into a ponytail before letting it fall free again. "I was just going to say that it's been a long time since I've been on a date. But you probably figured that out all on your own." Carmen laughed at herself and took a sip of water. "What were you going to say?"

He smiled, showcasing that amazingly gorgeous dimple. "I was just going to say that we make quite the pair since I haven't been on a real date in years. Which is probably why my brother was such a bully about having us go out."

Carmen blanched at his choice of words, but chose to ignore them.

The waitress came and delivered their drinks. When she left, Carmen lifted her glass of wine and held it out. "A toast then," she said. "To the non-daters's, non-date."

She'd thought he would laugh at her joke, or at least smile again, but instead his face flipped down into a frown. As she was taking a sip of her wine, Dylan put his beer down and examined her.

He stared at her for a long moment, deciding what to do. They were both obviously uncomfortable with the idea of dating, and she'd pretty much told him she didn't date. But looking at her, Dylan knew he wasn't going to let a little bit of insecurity on either of their parts ruin their night.

He was drawn to her, there was no doubt. Every time he looked at her, he felt this incredibly powerful urge to reach out and touch her. Take her hand in his and never let go. It didn't make sense, but there was something so compelling about her, he didn't know what to say or how to act. Which was apparent by his behavior up till that point.

"I'm sorry," he blurted out while she was taking another sip of her wine. "I can't toast to that." She lowered her glass and looked at him with a strange expression. Before he could change his mind, he pushed up from his chair and stood next to the table."

"Dylan, what—"

He held out one finger and said, "Don't go anywhere. Just give me thirty seconds. Please."

When she nodded, he turned and walked out of the restaurant. Once in the corridor of the main lodge, Dylan looked around frantically. Now what? He'd had this great, albeit poorly formed idea, but it would've been even better if he'd taken even a second to think it through.

Further down the hall was a gift shop. In the other direction was the lobby. Dylan racked his brain for something, anything he could do to show her that he wanted to be on a real date with her. But it had to be fast. He couldn't stand in the hallway all evening. She probably already thought he was crazy. If he didn't hurry, she'd leave altogether and he wouldn't get another chance. He sprinted to the gift shop, hoping on the off chance there might be a flower, or something that would pass for a first-date gift.

"Good evening," the girl behind the counter said.

He nodded in her direction and scanned the shelves.

"Can I help you find something?"

"Do you have flowers?"

"As in, fresh flowers?" The girl raised an eyebrow. "I have postcards of flowers, a package of wildflower seeds, and a—"

"But no flowers?"

She shook her head. "There's a little flower shop in the square, but it would have closed at five. They mostly do weddings and—"

"Never mind," he said, and then added, "Sorry. I'm not trying to be rude, but I need something for a first date and I was really hoping you'd have flowers."

"What about chocolate?"

"Yes." Dylan followed the girl down one of the crowded aisles and checked out the selection of gourmet maple syrup flavored treats. "This is all you have? Nothing in a box wrapped in a ribbon?"

"It's not Valentine's Day, sir."

He thought the girl was going to laugh at him, and really, if he wasn't in a panic that Carmen was at that very moment getting up from the table and walking out, he might have laughed at himself, too.

Dylan must have looked panicked, because the girl took pity on him. "Look," she said. "If I were you, I'd take two of these." She pointed to a few of the dark chocolates. "I can wrap them in some tissue for you. And if your date really likes flowers, why not give her one of those." She pointed to a display of stuffed toys, with some plush daisies with embroidered faces, sticking from the top of the rack. "They're kinda cute," she added.

"Done." Dylan snatched a gluey-green flower—the color reminded him of Carmen's eyes—and met the girl at the cash register where she was almost finished wrapping the chocolates. "Can you charge it to my room?"

"Of course."

He could barely stand still long enough to give her the

information and sign off on the receipt before he grabbed his purchases and darted back to the Grill.

To his relief, Carmen was still sitting at the table, her back to him as he forced himself to slow down and walk through the restaurant.

Dylan, play it cool, he told himself in an effort to slow down his thoughts. He took a deep breath as he approached the table and slid into his seat.

Carmen looked up from her glass of wine and the shock on her face was quickly replaced by a smile when she saw the goofy flower and small package in front of him.

"I should have given these to you earlier," Dylan said. He handed the gifts to her and was rewarded by the sweet sound of her laughter.

"What is this? You didn't have to—"

"Yes I did," he said. "On a proper first date, it's customary to bring flowers or chocolate."

"But, I—"

"You don't date," he said, ready for the objection. When she'd said that earlier, he'd chosen to ignore it. As a rule, Dylan didn't date either, but there was something about Carmen that was making him reconsider every self-imposed rule he'd ever placed upon himself and he was hoping she'd do the same. "But maybe you could pretend you do, just for tonight," he said. "And maybe, this could be a real first date."

She didn't object right away, but tipped her head and unwrapped the package. When she saw what was inside, she laughed again and Dylan joined in.

"I know it's not a box of chocolates or anything, and I would have preferred to get you roses or something, but I did the best I could with what I had to work with."

"It's perfect," she said. When she looked up into his eyes, they were full of humor and he knew he'd made the right choice. "Besides, I hate roses." She held up the stuffed flower.

"Daisies are my favorite. Especially blue ones. And how did you know that maple syrup chocolates are my weakness?"

"Just a guess."

The waitress chose that moment to reappear and take their orders.

"I haven't even had a chance to look at the menu," he said. "Assuming, you'd like to join me for dinner." He turned to Carmen.

She smiled and nodded. "I'd love to," she said, her eyes never leaving his. "After all, there is typically dinner on a proper first date, right?"

They stared at each other for a moment, forgetting the waitress was still standing there. It wasn't until she cleared her throat that he reluctantly took his eyes away from Carmen, who looked down and fidgeted with her napkin.

"What's your special tonight?" he asked.

"It's a beautiful pan seared—"

"I'll have that," Carmen said.

Dylan laughed. "Me too," he said.

The waitress shook her head, scribbled some notes on her pad and walked away.

"It doesn't matter what it is," Carmen said. "The food here is excellent. I know the chef, and he's never made me a meal I haven't enjoyed. Besides, she would have stood there all night if we didn't make a decision."

"I trust your decision." He reached out and in a bold move, covered her hand that was holding the flower. Her eyes flew up and met his, but she didn't move. "And I don't really care what it is, I'm just glad this is going better. Now that we've agreed that it is indeed a date."

There was a flicker of something in her eyes before she looked down at her lap, and for a moment Dylan thought maybe he'd pressed too hard. But when she looked up again, it was gone. He could stare all night at those amazing eyes, and watch the way they sparkled when she laughed. Never had he enjoyed just being with a woman. The only problem was it was a terrible time for him to get involved with anyone. Especially when he'd be returning to the Springs to get the resort ready for the opening date. He hardly had time to date anyone, let alone get involved with a relationship.

He pushed the thoughts out of his head and instead focused on the beautiful woman in front of him. It didn't matter if he had time or not; he'd think about that if and when it became an issue. For the moment, he didn't need or want any thoughts or responsibilities interrupting his evening. He was just going to enjoy every moment of her company.

Chapter Four

HALFWAY THROUGH HER second glass of wine, Carmen realized she wasn't just having a good time, she was genuinely enjoying herself. She'd also managed to completely forget the reason she was sitting there. Well, almost.

"Trent tells me you're up for his job when he leaves," Dylan said.

It was an innocent statement and probably made in an effort to make easy conversation, but it stopped Carmen cold. What else had Trent told Dylan?

"I'm probably not going to get it," she said cautiously. "It's kind of a long shot, really."

"That's not what I hear," Dylan said. "In fact, Trent said you're absolutely fantastic. So, if they're basing their hiring decision on merit, it sounds like you're a sure thing."

Carmen looked down and started fidgeting with her napkin. She folded the hem into an accordion pattern. "I guess we'll see," she said.

"There are other options if you don't get the job."

Something in his voice caused Carmen to look up again. "What do you mean?"

Dylan shrugged and glanced away. "I guess I was just wondering, if for some crazy reason you don't get the general manager position," he said, "what are you going to do?"

Carmen had never considered the possibility of what she'd do. Mostly because she'd assumed she wouldn't get the position so she'd just continue in the role she had. She shook her head slightly. "I don't understand," she said. "I'll just keep doing what I'm doing. Why wouldn't I?"

A strange look crossed his face, and in that instant, something about his expression reminded her of Trent. "I wasn't trying to start anything," Dylan said quickly. "I guess that was just my stupid way of asking you how long you planned on staying at the Lodge?"

When he smiled, and his boyish dimple reappeared, Carmen felt a wash of relief. Dylan was so different from his big brother, but that little glimpse was a little too similar for her liking. "I honestly haven't given it much thought," she said. "I like it here. But mostly, I like my career. I've always been really focused on getting ahead. It's all I've ever wanted."

"Really?"

"You sound surprised."

"I am a little bit. It's refreshing to meet a woman so driven." He rolled his beer bottle between his hands. "A lot of women I meet seem to be only interested in finding a husband. Preferably one with lots of money."

She laughed at the way he rolled his eyes. "Well then, you're hanging around the wrong sorts of women."

He looked directly in her eyes, and reached for her hand. A thrill shot through her but she tried not to show how he affected her with just one simple touch. "I plan on remedying that," he said, never losing eye contact.

They sat in silence for a minute, neither of them willing to look away first. Finally, Carmen knew she'd have to be the first to speak.

"Now it's your turn," she said. "Tell me something about you."

He smiled lazily and tipped his head. "What do you want to know?"

"Well, I know you have an older brother, who from what I can tell so far, is your complete opposite. I also know you're involved in business together. He's the management and you are the…"

"I'm the brains."

"Obviously." She smirked. "So tell me about your project. Trent hasn't mentioned much." Of course she hadn't asked, but she didn't bother telling Dylan that. "All I know from what the two of you have mentioned is that it's a resort in the mountains, centered around some hot springs."

Dylan took a long pull on his beer, leaned back and crossed his leg over his knee. "That's a pretty simplified view of it, but yes. Basically, I discovered these therapeutic hot springs a few hours west of here. Have you ever heard of a town called Cedar Springs?"

She shook her head.

"Neither had I," he said. "It's really just an old logging town with a handful of locals who are trying to hang on to their homes, but the really remarkable thing is that there's this amazing hot spring up in the hills. It's bigger than most of the springs around here, and there's actually three separate pools."

"Three?" Carmen leaned forward, genuinely interested.

"Three. And they're all grouped together," he said. "And there's some local folklore that says the water in the pools has healing properties. People have actually come from all over the world to soak in the pools and cure their diseases—arthritis, chronic fatigue, you name it."

"No way." Carmen leaned back as the waitress came and delivered their food to them. Neither of them touched their meals right away. Instead, Carmen asked, "Okay, well, if it's a world-famous pool, then how is it that the town isn't already overrun with tourists?"

Dylan smiled and crossed his arms over his chest. "That's the best part," he said. "The land was privately owned and up until recently, the rancher wouldn't allow anyone to access his land. Those who did want to soak in the springs had to do it late at night, and sneak in and out of the fence he'd put up. He was known for chasing people off his land with a shotgun on more than one occasion."

"No way."

"It's true," Dylan said. "Fortunately, he never actually shot anyone."

"No kidding." Carmen picked up her fork and started poking around at her meal, which looked to be a stuffed chicken breast with some sort of mashed vegetables. Her mouth watered at the aroma coming off it, and she could no longer resist whatever Bruno had created in the kitchen. "So," she said. "If the rancher was so dead set against letting anyone on to his land to use the pools, how on earth did you get a hold of it?" She sliced a piece of chicken and put it in her mouth.

Instead of answering her right away, he tipped his head and watched her for a moment. She should have been self-conscious with his eyes on her, but Carmen actually liked it. She smiled and took another bite of her meal.

"Looks good," he said, his voice low.

"It is. You should try some." She waved a piece of chicken around on her fork, teasing him with it. Dylan just laughed and took a bite of his own meal. The more time she spent with him, the more she realized how much she enjoyed that sound and just how awesome it was that he wasn't afraid to laugh, especially at himself.

She waited until he was done chewing the food in his mouth before she said, "You haven't told me yet how you got the land from the old rancher."

"He died," Dylan said simply.

Carmen almost choked on her water. "What? That's terrible."

"Well, it is and it isn't," he said with a shoulder shrug. "He was an old man and he passed away peacefully in his sleep. His son inherited all the land and fortunately for Trent and me, he didn't want anything to do with it. We got it for a good price and we're really excited about bringing the Springs resort to the town. I think it will be a huge boost to the local economy, provide a lot of jobs and with any luck at all, help a lot of people feel better."

He seemed so passionate about his project, Carmen couldn't help but get swept up in it. It would be nice to have such a strong passion for something. It was similar, she supposed, to the way she felt about her work at the Lodge. It was important to her to do a good job, to leave a mark. Whatever type of mark she could leave on a huge, well-established resort hotel. She pushed away the doubt and tried to refocus on her date. She was enjoying herself too much to let negative feelings creep in and ruin things.

"It sounds fabulous," she said, and meant it. "It must be really exciting to finally see it happening."

"It is." Dylan took another bite of his meal and dabbed at the corners of his mouth with a napkin. "This is fantastic," he said. "I can't remember the last time I had such a great meal."

"I told you, you can't go wrong with Bruno. He's the best chef in the Rockies."

"I wonder if he'd consider a move?"

Instinctively, Carmen bristled. He couldn't take Bruno from the Lodge. He belonged here. And not only that, the Lodge needed him. Events were booked months and sometimes years in advance based on Bruno's menus and availability. If the Harrison brothers thought they could steal Bruno, they'd have a fight on their hands. Carmen straightened in her chair. "I don't think Bruno would consider a change."

"What if the deal was right?" Dylan laid his napkin across his plate and locked eyes with her. "One thing I've discovered during my time in the business world is that people will do all kinds of things you didn't expect them to do. You'd be surprised."

He had no idea how close to home his comment hit, and she wasn't about to let him know. Hadn't she herself just agreed to something all for the sake of the promise of a new title and with it, more money?

Carmen shook her head. "No. It's not happening." She wished she felt as confident as she sounded. The truth was, she had no way of knowing if Bruno would take a different job offer or if his loyalty to the Lodge was as strong as she thought it was. "He wouldn't leave."

"Would you?"

The question was so pointed and so unexpected, Carmen didn't have a chance to think about her response before she said, "We're not talking about me."

She looked down at her plate, her appetite gone. Her stomach churned with the thought of Dylan and Trent poaching the staff from Castle Mountain Lodge. Was that really why Dylan was here? Was that why he was sitting with her, pretending to be on a date with her? She rubbed her temple and tried to clear her thoughts.

"Are you okay?" he asked. "Do you have a headache?"

Carmen looked up and met his concerned gaze. "You know what…I'm not feeling great all of a sudden. I should probably get going."

She stood to leave, but Dylan reached out and grabbed her hand. Her heart stopped for a second. He really had to stop touching her. She couldn't seem to form a coherent thought when the heat of his hand was on hers.

"I didn't mean it, Carmen." He looked so disappointed that for an instant, Carmen considered changing her mind. "I didn't mean it. I wouldn't try to steal Bruno from the Lodge," he said. "Or anyone. That's not the way I operate. I really hope I didn't give you the impression that I would do something like that because that's not how I choose to live my life or handle my business dealings. I'll always be straight with you."

The guilt swirled in her stomach, and for a moment, Carmen was afraid she'd be sick. "I believe you," she said, and she did. He looked so genuine it was hard to think he could lie to her.

"He's such a part of the Lodge," Dylan continued. "I wouldn't dream of trying to take that away."

"I said that I believed you," she said.

Dylan glanced down at their hands, still locked together. "Then why don't you sit?"

For a second, she considered it. But the unrelenting swirl in her stomach and the genuineness in Dylan's face made up her mind. She obviously wasn't thinking clearly where Dylan was concerned, and she needed a bit of space before she did or said something she might regret. And if he didn't let go of her soon, there was a very real chance of that. She wiggled her hand away from his.

"I really should be going," she said. "I'm not feeling very well and I totally forgot that my parents are coming in the morning and I need to make sure their room is all set up." It wasn't a lie. With everything that had happened with Dylan, she'd completely forgotten about her parents.

"I'd love to meet your parents," Dylan said.

She almost sat back down from the shock of it. "Um, no," she said. "I don't think so."

"Why not? I'd like to know more about you and there's no better way to get to know someone than by meeting their family."

"I really don't know, Dylan. They're only here for a short time and you don't know them. They can be quite...well, frustrating."

He chuckled. "I'm sure they're great." He squeezed her hand and Carmen knew in that touch that he felt the same connection between them. Which meant she was in trouble. He was gorgeous, smart, and made her smile more than she had in a very long time. But her instincts were telling her it wasn't a good idea to have any kind of relationship with Dylan Harrison, not if it meant she was going to feel the way she was feeling.

Carmen's instincts had never been wrong before and things with Dylan could only get complicated, especially if he wanted to meet her parents. The last thing she needed them thinking was that there was even the remotest chance that she was in an actual relationship. Especially since there wasn't even the remotest chance that she was going to allow herself to be in a relationship.

Dylan fought the urge to chase after Carmen. Instead, he stood, said good-night and let her leave. He surprised himself with how much he didn't want to see her go, but he was also smart enough to know when to step back. Something had spooked her. Maybe it was talking about the Springs, and what options she might have when it came to a job? Maybe it was their date itself? Whatever it was, it was definitely something he'd done or said. That much he knew for sure. Whatever he'd said about her parents, while maybe it was true, was not the real reason she'd fled. That much he knew for sure.

He shook his head and reached for his beer. A smart man would cut his losses right now and walk away. But despite all his business smarts, when it came to Carmen, Dylan was quickly figuring out that he was not a smart man. She was one of the most engaging women he'd had a pleasure to have dinner with.

A smile came to his lips as he thought of how passionate she got when he mentioned stealing Bruno for the Springs. He'd been kidding—well, mostly. But seeing her come alive and get fired up was worth it. At least it would have been if she hadn't left.

Dylan gestured to the waitress, who came over and cleared the plates.

"Can I get you anything else?" she asked and leaned in closely.

The smell of her perfume was overwhelming when she was so close. He pushed back, needing a bit of space. "Just a beer," he said.

She winked at him and left. Dylan shook his head, unsure of what had just happened. He pulled his cell phone out of his pocket. There were two missed calls, both from Trent and a text:

R u done? Is she on board?

Dylan sighed. There was no way he was going to ask Carmen about working for them now. Especially if it jeopardized whatever it was that was going on between them. He tapped in a message of his own:

Come for a beer at the Grill.

Trent had to be finished with the Braxtons or he wouldn't be harassing him. And that contract was more important than trying to steal Carmen away. Moments later, Dylan's phone buzzed with the message.

C U in 5

Dylan had just long enough to order Trent a beer of his own, and run through the events of his date with Carmen one more time before his brother showed up, still wearing his suit.

"Aw, you didn't have to dress up for me," Dylan said with a smirk.

Trent took his jacket off and slung it across the back of the chair. "Okay, smart ass. I didn't have time to go back to the apartment to change. Man, I'm not going to miss that staff accommodation," he said. Trent took a deep pull of his beer. "I can't wait until I can move into my own suite at the Springs. Please tell me the construction is almost finished."

"It is," Dylan said. "Don't worry about any of that. I told you I'd handle it." He didn't bother adding that he'd need the Braxton investment dollars if he was going to get the resort finished as planned. Trent knew things were tight, but he had no idea just how tight things were. And there wasn't any point worrying him about it. "So, were the Braxtons happy with the proposal?"

"They seemed to be." He put his half-empty beer down. "I'm going to need another one of these."

Dylan waved over the waitress again. "Sorry to bother you," he said. "But my brother here would like another beer."

The waitress bent low in front of Dylan, in a move that was not lost on him. "How about you?" she purred.

It took Dylan a moment to register the shift in the girl. She hadn't flirted at all with him while Carmen was sitting there; in fact, he'd hardly noticed her. But maybe, thinking back on it, she'd given him a few signals after Carmen had left, but either he was really out of practice, or just completely clueless since he hadn't picked up on it. It was probably the latter. "Sure," he said cautiously. "I'll have another."

"Coming right up." She backed away and winked before turning and wiggling her hips all the way to the bar.

Trent let out a low whistle. "Looks like someone has an admirer," he said.

"I'm not interested."

"You're kidding, right? That's Jessica, and I have it on good authority that she—"

"Doesn't matter. I'm not interested." Dylan held up a hand to ward off his brother's explanations on what exactly made Jessica so special. "I don't have time to date," he said. He flashed back to Carmen and the conversation they'd had about their non-date. If she gave him the chance, he may have to reconsider his policy.

But hadn't he already? Dylan rolled the beer bottle between his hands and remembered the way she'd smiled when he handed her the flower and chocolates. Her face lit up with the goofy gifts. The distinctly first-date gifts. Things with Carmen were becoming way too complicated for a situation that was supposed to be simple. But complicated or not, he couldn't help himself. He wanted to spend more time with her. He just had to convince her of that.

"Earth to Dylan." Trent waved a hand in front of his face. "Hello."

"What? I was just thinking."

"About Jessica?"

"No." Dylan tipped his beer back, draining it.

"Whatever," Trent said, dismissing him. "Did you secure Carmen?"

Dylan sat up and put both hands on the table. "Pardon me?"

"Whoa, calm down." Trent held up both hands and raised his eyebrows as if his brother had totally lost his mind. "I meant did you secure her for the Springs. Weren't you supposed to be taking care of that for me tonight? You did say you'd ask her, didn't you?"

Embarrassed, Dylan looked down at the tablecloth and fidgeted with the coffee spoon.

"You did ask her, didn't you, Dyl?"

"Not really."

"Not really? What the hell does that mean?"

"I didn't have a chance."

"Over dinner? You didn't have a chance to ask a simple question?"

"We were busy talking about other things."

"Oh," Trent said, dragging out the word. "I see what's happening here."

"No you don't."

"Oh, yes I do." Trent sat back and crossed his arms over his chest. "You like her."

Dylan matched his posture, but couldn't find the words to protest the truth. Instead, he stared at his older brother, challenging him to look away first.

Jessica returned with two new beers. She sat them down in front of the men, raised her eyebrows and retreated without saying anything.

After a minute, Trent shook his head. "There's nothing wrong with that," he said. "As long as you know it's not going to last."

"I thought you wanted me to go out with her." Dylan eyed his brother suspiciously. "And that's all we're doing."

"That's good," Trent said and took a swig of his beer. "Because you're right, I did want you to go out. I wanted you to have a little fun, stop working for a few minutes. Have a fling. That's why I suggested Carmen. She doesn't date. I thought maybe she'd be interested in a fling too."

"I don't do flings."

"Well, you don't do relationships."

Dylan picked up his beer and examined the table. "Neither of us does," he said quietly.

"And for good reason, little brother. I taught you well."

"You taught me something alright." Dylan rolled his eyes when his brother wasn't looking but he couldn't stop thinking about what Trent had just said. He suggested Carmen? What did that mean? Carmen had asked him out.

Trent narrowed his eyes and regarded his brother. "Why do I get the impression there's more to this? You like her, don't you?"

"Trent," Dylan warned.

"That's it, isn't it? You like her." Trent slammed his beer down on the table. "Leave it to you to screw up a fling."

"It's not a fling and—"

"But you like her."

"Drop it," Dylan growled.

Trent opened his mouth to say more, and for a moment, Dylan thought he might have to remind his brother that although he might be older, he was not stronger. Wisely, Trent shut his mouth and opted for another taste of his beer.

"I've gotta go," Dylan said. He abruptly pushed away from the table and stood. The room was too hot to sit in. He had to move, had to get some fresh air and clear his head. He had too much going on to let his thoughts get clouded by a woman.

"You invited me."

Dylan didn't bother arguing with him. He threw some money on the table and left. Without thinking about where he was going, he walked to the end of the corridor, and straight out the doors into what looked to be a bricked courtyard area. He hadn't had time to explore the Lodge fully, and who was he kidding, he still hoped Carmen would be able to show him around. In fact, he'd looked forward to the prospect of seeing the sights with a beautiful woman by his side. Trent didn't need to know what he may or may not be feeling towards Carmen. Especially since Dylan couldn't figure it out himself.

The courtyard was lit with only a few lanterns hanging from the trees. His eyes adjusted to the dim light and he started walking. The space held a few benches and tables that looked like they'd been put there for picnics or card games among the guests. As he walked, the space narrowed into a path that led to a pond, with a rocky waterfall at one end. It was just far enough away from the main lodge to be quiet, and he could only barely see the lights from the main building, but the few lanterns there were provided enough glow that he wasn't sitting in complete darkness.

He picked his way up the rocks, to a flat boulder where he could sit close to the water but not get wet. The sound of the water flowing over the stones into the pool below soothed him, as he was sure it was intended to do. Dylan leaned back on his hands and gazed up at the stars that covered the night sky in a splatter. The only other place he'd seen such a display was in Cedar Springs.

There were a lot of similarities to the two places, but as much as he was enjoying Castle Mountain Lodge, Dylan pictured the Springs differently. It would be more serene, with a spa-like atmosphere. The environment would promote healing, both spiritual and physical. It would be a focus on the individual self, not the way the Lodge focused on couples. The perfect place for a man who avoided relationships.

From everything Trent had told him, Castle Mountain was gaining a reputation for love. More and more weddings were being booked, and couples were escaping to the mountains to rekindle the spark that daily life may have eroded. And he'd heard his share of stories about love discovered at the Lodge, too. So why hadn't Carmen found love? The thought popped into his head before he knew it.

He ran one hand through his hair and tried to focus again on the Springs, but it was no use. Carmen occupied his every thought. Her piercing eyes that held so much depth. He wanted to know everything she was thinking. Every guarded secret she held. Never had a woman captivated him so completely. He wanted to know more. No, he needed to know more.

Dylan picked up a loose pebble and tossed it into the water. Up until an hour ago, he'd actually thought he might be able to have that chance. Even if it was a purely platonic relationship and she allowed him to take her up on her original offer to show him around, he'd take it. After all, he wasn't lying when he'd told Trent he didn't do flings. He didn't. For him, it was all or nothing with women, which is why it was almost always nothing. He picked up another pebble and threw it in, watching the ripples along the water. The problem was, every time he was within a foot of Carmen, all he wanted to do was pull her into his arms and claim her mouth with his. And that was hardly platonic.

Chapter Five

CARMEN PUT a cup of coffee in front of Morgan and slipped in to her own seat across from her at the small table in the lobby. They'd claimed two wing backed chairs in a quiet corner in front of one of the windows. Far enough away from the front desk business, and yet still within sight of the door since Carmen was expecting her guests to show up within the hour. After ending their date the night before so abruptly, she'd spent all her waking hours, and even some of her sleeping ones, thinking of nothing but Dylan Harrison. And she'd only come up with one conclusion—she needed advice from a friend.

"Thank you for meeting me here," Carmen said. "I know it would have been nicer to meet anywhere else. I feel like I spend my whole life in this room."

Morgan laughed. "It's a good thing it's so beautiful in here then." She added a packet of sugar to her coffee. "Seriously, it's no problem. I understand."

"If I missed my parents' arrival, I'd never hear the end of it." Carmen shook her head and added her own sugar. "Trust me, this is a small price to pay. And I did want to talk to you about something."

Morgan stirred her coffee and leaned forward. "This sounds juicy," she said. "Do tell."

"Relax. It's not that big of a deal." That was a lie, Carmen thought, but didn't say. It was a big deal; at least, for her it was. All she'd been able to think of was Dylan Harrison with his disarming smile and the way her body thrilled when he touched her.

"It wouldn't happen to be about Trent Harrison's little brother by chance, would it?"

Carmen did a second take at her friend, who was trying unsuccessfully not to smile. "How did you—"

"Astrid." Morgan smiled apologetically. "She mentioned that you were going on a date. So of course I had to know all the details."

"It wasn't a date."

Her friend tipped her head and raised her eyebrows. "Okay," Carmen admitted. "It was sort of a date. But like I said, it's no big deal."

"By the look on your face, I'd say it's a big deal." Morgan took a sip of her drink. "A very big deal. Now spill."

There was no point putting it off. After all, that was the whole point of asking Morgan to meet her. She desperately needed some sense knocked into her. She took a deep breath. "Have you met Trent's brother yet?"

Morgan shook her head. "Up until yesterday I didn't even know he had a brother."

Carmen nodded. "Well, he does. Obviously. Anyway, he's here right now for some business meetings for that new resort they're opening."

"Oh yes," Morgan said. "I do remember Bo saying something about that. They're developing some hot springs or something."

"That's it." Carmen tasted her coffee, trying to calm herself. "And as you've heard, I've had the pleasure of meeting

Dylan." That was putting it mildly, she thought. "He's very…nice."

"Nice?" Morgan raised her eyebrows.

"And handsome."

"Ahh, and there it is," Morgan said, with a smile. "The real reason for our little coffee date today."

Carmen dropped her head into her hands. "Yes. It's terrible."

Morgan had been taking a sip of her own coffee and for a second, Carmen thought her friend might choke on it. She sat up in her chair and waited while Morgan got a hold of herself. "Terrible?" Morgan repeated, when she regained control. "Why on earth would meeting a handsome man be terrible? It's about time you met someone."

"Because I've told you a million times, I don't want a relationship." Carmen stared at her friend as if she had suddenly sprouted a tail. "Seriously, do you ever listen to me?"

Morgan waved a hand in Carmen's direction. "Cut it out. You know I listen to you. Now tell me what's really going on. And you better make it quick, because if your parents show up, I get the feeling you won't really feel like sharing this bit of information with them, too."

"Ugh." Carmen dropped her head to the table. "My parents are a whole separate problem." She sat up. "But I really can't think about that right now. I need your help with Dylan." Morgan made a motion with her hand that basically told Carmen to spit it out. "I think I like him."

"And that's a problem, how?"

Carmen closed her eyes for a moment, debating on how much she should tell her friend about Trent's offer. In the end, the need to confide in someone won out.

"Well, besides the fact that I don't have any time at all for a relationship right now, I may have agreed to go out with him as a sort of favor."

"A sort of favor?"

Carmen leaned across the table and lowered her voice. "Trent asked me to take Dylan out as a favor. Something about him working too hard and needing to have some fun before things got crazy with the Springs. The thing is," Carmen swallowed hard before continuing, "he kind of told me if I did it, I would have a better chance at getting the manager job."

Morgan's hand flew to her mouth. "He did not."

Carmen nodded.

"Like a prostitute?"

"Oh my God, Morgan. No!" She took a quick look around to see if anyone had overheard. She lowered her voice and added, "It's not like that at all. Trent just asked me to take him out. Show him around the Lodge a little."

Morgan gave her a sidelong glance and took another sip of her coffee. "I honestly can't believe you agreed to that."

"I know." Carmen dropped her head into her hands and rubbed at her temple. "But honestly, he didn't give me much of a choice and I guess I didn't see what the harm was."

"But now?"

"Now I think I might like Dylan," she mumbled.

"And you don't want him to find out and think it was all fake," Morgan guessed.

Carmen looked up into her friend's eyes and nodded.

"So tell him," Morgan said. "If you want to see where things could go with him, be honest. Nothing good can come from keeping secrets if you want to be together. But I don't get it, Carmen. Didn't you just say you were too busy for a relationship? Not that I don't think it's awesome you're interested in someone, but if it's not going to be serious, does it really matter?"

Carmen shrugged and fiddled with the handle on her mug. "So honesty," she said. "Or say nothing?"

"I think it depends on what you want. There's probably no harm in it if you never plan on seeing him again."

"Awesome." Carmen rolled her eyes.

"Sorry I can't be more help," Morgan said. "But for the record, I'm all for a relationship." She smiled and Carmen recognized the glow in her friend's face. It'd been there since she and Bo finally made their own relationship official and moved in together. She couldn't help but feel a twinge of envy. It might be nice to have that, too.

A commotion at the front door caught her eye and she sighed. "You're not the only ones who'd be happy with me in a relationship." She nodded towards the entrance where her mom and dad were busy turning down the efforts of the bellboy while simultaneously arguing with each other as they dragged their suitcases into the lobby. "Here comes the heads of the 'marry Carmen off' committee now."

Morgan laughed. "I'm sure they're not that bad."

Carmen raised her eyebrows, causing Morgan to laugh harder.

"Maybe you should introduce them to Dylan," Morgan suggested between giggles. "At least that way they'd think you were settling down."

"Right." Carmen stood and straightened her blouse. "And they'd be planning the wedding before they even left. No thanks." She turned to Morgan and gave her a quick hug. "Thanks for the chat. Now, wish me luck."

"You got it."

Carmen loved her parents; she really did. And she reminded herself of that fact as she crossed the lobby towards them. She'd hoped to head them off before they got to the check-in desk, but her mother had beaten her to it.

"We have a very important reservation," her mother was saying to Joe, the customer service clerk on duty. "If you look it up, it should be under Carmen Kincaid. That's K-I-N-"

"I got it, Mom." Carmen flashed an apologetic smile to Joe, who grinned back and turned to the next guest.

"Carmen." Her mother turned to her and frowned. "We expected you to meet us."

"I am meeting you, Mom. I'm here, in the lobby."

"Well, you could have—"

"You look good, kid," her dad said. Carmen turned and let her dad hug her. It didn't matter how old she got, or how long it'd been, nothing felt better than a hug from her dad.

"She looks too thin," her mother said.

"Thanks, Mom." Carmen stepped out of her dad's arms and grabbed an envelope she'd slid into a drawer behind the desk earlier. "I already checked you in. Come on, I'll take you up to your room so you can get settled."

"Did you get us the suite?" her mom asked. "I was really hoping we could stay in one of those fancy suites like where Gage Mitchell stayed when he was here. Bill, he was the star of *Extinction*. And that new Western show. I can never remember the names of these—"

"*Tumbleweed*," Carmen supplied.

"Tumble-what?"

"*Tumbleweed*," Carmen repeated. "That's the name of the show."

Her mother waved her hand. "Whatever. It doesn't matter. Did you get us one of those suites? I hear they're quite fancy and have their own living rooms and—"

"Linda, I'm sure whatever room Carmen got us will be fine," her father interrupted. "We're just happy to be here, kiddo. It's been too long."

Carmen grabbed the handle of a suitcase and started walking towards the elevator bank. "It has been awhile." She tried not to do a mental countdown of how many hours she had left in their visit, but the idea of spending some time with

Dylan and away from her family was becoming more and more appealing by the second.

———

Dylan forced himself to focus on the task at hand, which at that moment was dealing with his general contractor. He glanced one more time out the window at the sunny fall day. He'd been in his makeshift office, an empty boardroom that Trent had given him to use, since six a.m. He'd already decided to work at least until one o'clock before taking a break because he knew exactly where that break would take him, and once he found Carmen, he was pretty sure he wouldn't be returning to the office. At least that was his hope.

With a sigh, he pushed thoughts of Carmen out of his mind for the moment and dialed the number for Jake Mentz, his head contractor working on the Springs, returning his call. He already knew what Jake was going to want. The same thing he'd been wanting to know for the last few weeks—when he was going to get paid. And Dylan would have an answer for him, too. Just as soon as Trent showed up with the signed contract from the Braxtons. But Dylan couldn't put off the call any longer.

The phone rang only once before Jake picked up.

"Harrison."

"Hey, Jake. Sorry it's taken me a few days to get back to you. I've been trying to get some answers about that issue we were talking about."

"By issue, you mean my paycheck?"

Jake never minced words, which is one of the things Dylan had liked about him from the beginning.

"That's pretty much it."

"Tell me some good news then, Harrison. I have a whole

crew that's looking to get paid here next week and I can't keep sitting on promises."

Dylan rubbed the bridge of his nose. He had two choices. He could tell Jake the truth, that the funds were close, but not confirmed. Or he could take a gamble that Jake would take his crew off the job and walk out. Well," he said after a moment. "I have good and bad news."

"That doesn't sound like what I want to hear, Harrison."

Dylan sighed. "I'm sorry, Jake. The good news is, the investor is closer than ever to signing."

"But?"

"He hasn't yet." Dylan braced himself for the contractor's response.

There was silence, and then Jake said, "You know I'll have to stop work, Harrison. I'm sorry."

Dylan was afraid of that. The promise of money was just not the same as actual money. "I get it, Jake. I do. It should only be a day or two at most," he added.

"Let me know, Harrison. As soon as you have the funds, I'll get my guys back on the job. But—"

"I know." Dylan ran a hand through his hair, tugging on the roots. "I'll talk to you soon."

He hung up the phone and Dylan looked out the window in an effort to slow his thoughts. He needed to secure the Braxtons and fast. If Trent found out work had stopped on the Springs, it wouldn't go over well. He hated to lie to him, but maybe he could just avoid the topic altogether and as soon as the Braxtons signed, everything would be back to normal. Trent better come through with the contract because without it the Springs was in real trouble. Not to mention himself. He picked up the phone and pushed the button for Trent.

Three rings and the call went to voicemail.

"Trent. It's me. I forgot to ask you last night about the contract." Dylan could have kicked himself after he stormed out of the restaurant and hadn't even checked with Trent on the status of the most important business deal they'd ever had pending. Carmen was becoming too much of a distraction. This was why he didn't get involved with relationships. They caused nothing but trouble.

Dylan shook his head and focused on the task at hand.

"I need to know where we stand with the Braxtons," he said into the phone. "It's crucial that we have an answer and the funds by tomorrow at the latest. Call me back right away."

He hung up the phone and pushed up from his chair, choosing instead to pace in front of the window, not like it was going to help.

If they didn't get the investment dollars, the entire project would be compromised and Dylan would need to do some quick maneuvering to keep it from going under altogether.

Suddenly, the room was too warm. He unbuttoned the top button on his shirt and looked at his watch. It was only eleven o'clock, but he'd had enough. He couldn't stand around and worry. It wouldn't do any good and until he heard back from Trent, there really was no point in carrying on with anything else. He couldn't shake the nagging feeling that he had something else he was supposed to do, but he couldn't focus on a damn thing anyway. He closed up his laptop and stuffed his things into his case. He was done.

He knew he could probably find Trent in his office, and that probably should have been where he was headed, but he couldn't think straight and there was only one person responsible for that. And only one person who would be able to cure it.

Dylan took a chance and headed for the lobby, since that's where Carmen seemed to spend most of her time, even when she wasn't working.

Sure enough, just as he'd guessed, he spotted her dark hair bent over the reservation desk. She wasn't wearing her uniform, which he took as a good sign. Maybe he could convince her to take off for the afternoon.

"Hi."

She jerked her head up, but he was rewarded by the smile he loved so much when she realized it was him.

"Hi," she said. "I'm glad to see you."

His heart sped up a little. Maybe he wasn't the only one whose thoughts were completely occupied by the other.

"Really?"

"Yes, I wanted to apologize for last night," she said. "I shouldn't have taken off like that. I just…well, I'm sorry."

"Don't worry about it." He leaned on the desk and resisted the urge to reach out and touch her face. "Maybe you can make it up to me?"

She smiled, but gave him a questioning look. "Shouldn't you be working?"

"Probably." He shrugged. "But I don't have any meetings today and I was sitting in one of those boardrooms in the back getting a few things done, but I kept getting distracted."

"Oh, yeah?" She tilted her head and her hair fell like a wave over her shoulder. "By what?"

Dylan propped an elbow on the desk, and looked into her eyes. "It's such a beautiful day, and all I could think about was spending it outside with you."

She didn't immediately object, which Dylan took to be a good sign. In fact, there was a glint in her eye and she said, "Did you really?"

Encouraged, he leaned in. "I did. In fact, that's all I've been able to think about for the last few hours. And I believe you told me there was a lot to do up here in the mountains. How about you show me what Castle Mountain Lodge has to offer?"

She didn't say anything right away and Dylan noticed the hesitation that clouded her eyes. She looked down and tapped her pen on her desk. After what seemed like a very long time, she looked up and said, "As a matter of fact, it would be a perfect day to visit Crown Lake. They'll be putting the boats away for the season soon, but it would be lovely out there today."

"Boats? Let's do it." He grinned. A day in a boat with Carmen would be exactly what he needed to take his mind off the Springs and the precarious situation he was in.

"Oh, there's just one thing." Carmen's face clouded for a minute, her smile fading. "My parents are here."

Dylan stood up and stretched his neck. "That's right," he said. "You did say they were coming. What are they up to today?" He had a feeling he was going to regret the question.

Carmen flinched. He'd gotten the impression the night before that she wasn't overly excited about their visit, but he'd just assumed she was overreacting the way most people did when they had to entertain family members.

"You may have noticed I'm not working today?" She gestured down to her jeans and sweater. "I took the day off and promised to spend some time with them, so..."

"Oh, I see," he said with a straight face. "So that's why you're standing behind the desk instead of hanging out with them?" He couldn't resist teasing her a little. He grinned and she shot him a look, but returned his smile. "It's okay," Dylan added. And before he knew what he was saying, he added, "Why don't you see if they're interested in a boat ride. It could be fun."

"Seriously?" She tilted her head and blinked at him as if he'd just suggested they all go to the moon and back. "You just busted me working on my day off in order to avoid them, and you're really offering to take them out to the lake?"

Yes, he thought. He was definitely going to regret it. But more than anything, he wanted to spend time with Carmen, and the alternative—going back to the boardroom to stress about money he didn't have—was just not appealing enough to make him change his mind. "Yes," he said. "I guess that's exactly what I'm offering."

"Okay," she said slowly. Her face lightened, and Dylan was rewarded with a grin. "Let's do it. Why not?"

Carmen called up to her parents' room and told them about the plan while Dylan went to change. He turned his phone off and stuffed it in his back pocket. There were a million reasons he should keep it on and wait for Trent's call, but there was one very good reason to ignore it. And she was waiting in the lobby.

By the time he returned to the lobby, Linda and Bill Kincaid were already there and anxiously awaiting their departure. It took Dylan only five minutes to determine that her parents were nice people who simply wanted to see their daughter more often. It was also easy to see how frustrated Carmen got with them, and he decided to make it his mission to make sure all three of them enjoyed their afternoon on the lake as much as he planned to. Dylan figured if he could keep her parents happy and entertained, maybe he'd win a few more points with Carmen and maybe he'd finally be able to sneak in a kiss later on, since all Dylan could think of when he looked at her was how good her full lips would feel on his.

"Dylan, would you mind driving the Jeep for me?"

"Of course." He tried to focus on what she was saying about the rough roads, and the tight trails, but it was impossible to concentrate on anything when she looked at him like that, and stood so close, and smelled so damn good. He took the keys from her hand and let his fingers brush along the sensitive skin on the inside of her wrist. "I'd love to drive," he said.

She swallowed hard and looked away. "Good. I've never been comfortable on the bumpy roads. We should get going."

He grabbed her arm before she could slip away.

"Carmen?"

She turned and looked down at his hand gripping her arm.

"I just wanted to..." Dylan couldn't think of a thing to say, and he certainly couldn't kiss her, which is what he really wanted to do, with her parents standing only a few feet away. "Tell you I was looking forward to the lake," he finished lamely.

Her lips curled up into a smile. "Me too."

"Are you kids ready to go?" Bill came up behind them and Dylan pulled his hand away from Carmen.

"We're ready," Carmen said.

The drive didn't take long and Linda chatted the whole way, asking Carmen questions from the back seat about the trees, and potential wildlife they might see. Dylan was impressed with how much Carmen knew, but then again if she'd made Castle Mountain Lodge her home for the last few years, it wasn't surprising. She really did seem to love it. A flash of guilt crossed his mind as he remembered his promise to his brother about asking Carmen to move to the Springs and work for them. He'd also promised her he wasn't going to poach any of the staff. He couldn't very well go back on his promise in the biggest way possible by poaching her. He glanced across the seat to Carmen, who was pointing out some type of tree to her mother. But it would be nice if she was at the Springs. Maybe he'd have to reconsider his whole stance on dating and relationships. Dylan almost laughed out loud at the idea, because the more time he spent with her, the more he realized he'd been reconsidering from the moment he'd met her.

"Just pull over there," Carmen said. "By the hut. The life-jackets and paddles are inside the boathouse."

Dylan did as directed and soon they were all standing next to the Jeep, looking at the amazing scene in front of them.

"Carmen, how come we've never been up here before?" Linda asked as she stared open-mouthed at the lake.

The water was a cool green color that matched Carmen's eyes almost perfectly. Dylan also knew the color of the water meant that it was going to be very cold. The lake itself wasn't very big, and mountains completely surrounded it, giving it a secretive feeling. Despite the look of it, Dylan could tell it would take a good effort to paddle all the way across. Although he was game to give it a shot. The mountain on the far end of Crown Lake was covered in ice and snow. It must be the very same glacier that fed the lake and the streams below.

"This is amazing," he said. "It's so still." He walked to the water's edge and peered in. "You can see clear to the bottom. It's almost like it isn't real. Amazing."

Carmen came up next to him. "It's one of my favorite places," she said. "I don't get up here nearly as much as I'd like. It's especially nice at this time of year because there's barely anyone here. And the larch trees are all changing color." She pointed to the hills that were dotted with trees that looked like pines, but were a vibrant shade of yellow. She looked around and took a deep breath. "And today, it looks like we're the only ones out here. Shall we go get the boats?"

They all followed as Carmen led them to the boathouse and unlocked the door. They all suited up in life jackets, and Dylan handed everyone a paddle. Linda paused and shook her head slightly when he held one out to her.

"I don't think I can," she said. "I thought it would be a motorboat. I don't know about paddling."

"Mom." Carmen sighed. "It's a glacier lake in the middle of the mountains. There are no motors allowed. Besides, that's not the point. The whole idea is to enjoy the peace and quiet. If you don't want to go, you can stay here and—"

"No, no." Linda shook her head. "I want to go. Of course I want to go. Don't be silly, Carmen. I was just saying—"

"Here's your paddle." Dylan handed her the oar before she could object and they all headed outside to the canoe rack.

"We can fit two per boat," Carmen said. She looked over

the group, obviously unsure as to how to split them up, so Dylan jumped in before anyone else could make the decision.

"How about you take Linda out," Dylan said to Bill. He leaned in, and whispered, "It could be kind of romantic, don't you think?"

Bill gave him a wink and a nudge in the ribs, and a few minutes later, the canoes were in the water and they were off.

Chapter Six

CARMEN WASN'T sure how Dylan had convinced her mom and dad to share a boat, but she could have kissed him for giving her the gift of a few minutes away from them and their constant barrage of questions about her life. She couldn't even begin to imagine the inquisition she'd get about Dylan. So far they hadn't said anything about his presence, which in itself was a small miracle. Carmen knew they hadn't accepted Carmen's explanation of the two of them being work friends and she knew the questions were coming. And knowing her mom, she'd already started planning the wedding.

She looked across the canoe at Dylan, who'd insisted on doing all the rowing. He'd stripped off his sweater, warmed from the heat of the sun and the effort of his exertion. She admired him for a moment, and it really was admiration. He'd handled her parents so well, not giving them any opportunity to make her crazy. And he was so easy to be around. She was suddenly very thankful that Trent had bullied her into taking his brother out. The fact that Morgan was right, and she'd need to tell Dylan the truth before things went any further, was just a small detail. But she didn't want to think about it. At least not yet.

"What are you thinking?" he asked her. He lifted the paddle out and let the boat glide, cutting through the stillness of the water.

"I'm just thinking about how much I owe you for this," she said, giving him the half-truth. "And you didn't have to do all the paddling, you know. These canoes are meant for the effort of two people. And I'm not afraid of a little work."

"I know." He dipped the oar back into the water, and with a smooth stroke, propelled them forward again. "And I'm sure you'd be amazing at it. But if you were paddling too, I wouldn't be able to look at you, would I?"

She laughed and shook her head. "No, I suppose not."

"And you are definitely the most beautiful thing out here."

"Aren't you full of all the good lines, today?"

He grinned. "I'm learning," he said. "Is it working?"

"A little." Carmen dipped her head and smiled, enjoying how good it felt to flirt with him. "What else have you got?"

Instead of feeding her another line, Dylan kept quiet and gazed out over the water. "It really is amazing up here," he said after a moment. "Thank you for bringing me."

"I'm really glad it worked out," she said. "I wasn't sure what I was going to do with my parents, and really, they haven't even been here twenty-four hours and I'm already ready to kill them. I love my mom and dad, but sometimes I just wish they'd just…" She drifted off as she gazed over the lake to where her parents were paddling along the shoreline. Her mom seemed to have gotten over the fear of putting in a little effort with the oar. They'd bickered a little at first, but now they were cruising along, and although Carmen couldn't hear what they were saying, she could tell they were having a good time.

"What?" Dylan prompted.

"I don't know," she finished. "I really do love them. It just gets harder and harder when they come to visit because they won't take no for an answer. And it doesn't matter what I say, they don't seem to understand why I've made the choices I've made."

"What choices have you made?"

"This," she said, raising her arms to encompass their surroundings. "I chose all this, and the Lodge, instead of going to school, or more importantly to them, getting married and having a family. They think the most important thing for a woman is to get married and have babies. They've never understood why I wanted to have a career. And don't even get them started about my career in the hospitality industry. They think working at a hotel is a summer job type of thing, not a long-term career." She sighed and stared out over the water.

"But you love it."

It wasn't a question, but a statement and Carmen nodded. "I do." She turned back to Dylan, who seemed to be listening intently. Carmen couldn't remember the last time she'd spoken to anyone about her life who'd actually seemed to care about what she was saying. "The funny thing is, I originally came up to Castle Mountain to get away because I didn't know what I wanted to do with my life. All I knew was that I couldn't keep doing what I was doing, which was nothing really. My parents just assumed I was waiting for life to happen to me. And by life…they meant a man. I didn't know what I wanted, but I knew what I didn't want. So I left."

"And you didn't want a man?" He grinned, but Carmen could see there was more to the question.

"It's not that I didn't want one," she said. "It just wasn't all I wanted."

Dylan nodded. "Fair enough."

"Is it fair?"

"Of course." Dylan stopped paddling again and put the

oar up so it was crosswise over the boat. "It's all about what you want, Carmen. There's no right or wrong way to live your life. No set of rules you need to follow in order to do it properly."

"My mom and dad would disagree with you." She dipped her fingertips into the water and let them create a trail as the boat kept gliding along.

"That's because it's all they know," he said.

He spoke so softly that Carmen knew there was more behind his words than he was saying. "What about you, Dylan? What's your family like?"

She realized she'd been so caught up in her own family and own troubles, she hadn't even asked him. She didn't know much at all about Dylan, and she genuinely wanted to know more.

Dylan looked at her and raised his eyebrows before picking up the paddle and dipping it back into the water. "Every family has their own thing," he said. "You bucked the trend and did something different from how you were raised and what your folks wanted…I didn't."

"What do you mean?" She lifted her fingers from the water and wrapped them in the hem of her sweater to warm them up.

"My dad was Mister Business," Dylan continued. He didn't look at her, but seemed to focus on a point on the shore behind her. "Marriage—or relationships of any kind, really—weren't important to him. I think he's on his fourth or fifth wife now. I lost count after number three."

There was a pinch in Carmen's chest as she listened to him speak about his family. He wouldn't admit it, but there was a pain behind his words that she could sense. The urge to reach across the boat and hug him was strong, but she held herself back. She couldn't be sure he'd be receptive to that, and anyway there was a very real chance they'd both end up in the lake if she moved too much. Instead, she asked, "What about your mom?"

"She was wife number one. When I was six and Trent was seven, she left him after he went on a three-month business trip without even consulting her."

"Really?"

"It wasn't the first time. Basically, he treated us like a stopover between trips. But he couldn't be bothered to be a dad. It's not like we missed him after we left."

"Dylan, I'm so sorry."

"Don't be." He still wouldn't look at her or meet her eyes. "It's just the way it was. No reason to be upset or happy about it. It just was."

"Dylan." Carmen didn't care about the risk of capsizing; at that moment, she just cared about making contact with him, and healing the hurt he was so obviously feeling. She scooted forward, shifting her weight so she was kneeling on the floorboards and could put her hands on his knees. Still, he didn't stop paddling. "Dylan," she said again. She squeezed his knees, forcing him to look at her.

"You're going to tip us."

"I don't care."

"It's freezing."

"I don't care," she said again. "Look at me."

He did, and the pain he was trying to hide from her made her heart ache. "It's okay to be hurt about your past," she said softly.

"I can't change it."

"No. You can't. But you can learn from it. What did you mean, you did what your family wanted? What did they want you to be?"

"My dad wanted me to be like him," he said simply. "Mister Business."

"And your mom?"

"She died of uterine cancer when I was twelve. Trent and I went to live with Dad and wife number three."

"Dylan, I—"

"It doesn't matter, Carmen. You can't change it."

"I'm not trying to change it," she said. "I'm trying to understand."

He laid the paddle down and took her hands so she would get up off her knees. Carefully, Carmen shifted back on her heels so she was sitting down, but still she wouldn't move back to her bench. "I'm not trying to be difficult, Carmen. But I came to peace with my life a long time ago. When Trent and I went to live with Dad, he was still the same as he'd always been. More focused on work and building an empire than anything else. A strong work ethic was all he respected and as long as we did well in school, he was happy. The minute I graduated from college, he told me to get out on my own and make my way. The only advice he ever gave me was to create my own success and never to consider marriage or a family,— they'd only hold me back from that success. He encouraged both Trent and I to stay bachelors. So we did."

Carmen shook her head, trying, but failing, to understand. "So just like that, you decided not to get involved with anyone? Not to love?"

He shrugged. "More or less. Honestly, it wasn't a hard determination to come to. After all, we'd grown up with his example. All marriage did was cost him money. With every wife who divorced him, his alimony payments just went up. He didn't love any of those women. Well, except for maybe my mother. I do believe that at least at one point, he loved her."

Anger boiled in Carmen's core for the man she'd never met who could possibly ruin Dylan for the possibility of love and happiness. It didn't seem to matter that she herself had sworn off marriage and commitment, because she'd made her choices for much different reasons. It wasn't because she didn't think that a relationship could work. It was because she didn't think it could work for *her*. She couldn't be a successful woman in her own right if she was tied down to a man. But wasn't that exactly what Dylan was saying?

"No," she said aloud.

"No?" Dylan raised his eyebrows and examined her. "I really do think he loved her; he just didn't know how to show it."

"That's not what I meant," she said. "Sorry." Carmen looked out and found her parents' boat across the lake, still paddling along. "I think you're wrong about not being able to find love and success at the same time." She spoke so softly that she wasn't sure she'd even spoken aloud, but the look on Dylan's face confirmed it.

"Then why don't you believe that?" He slid the paddle down into the boat and moved forward, coming off the bench, so he, too, was sitting on the bottom of the canoe.

"I think my opinion may be changing," she whispered.

Dylan leaned forward, causing the boat to rock and Carmen gripped the sides. He was so close she could feel the heat coming off his body. She wanted to reach out and tuck her hands under his shirt to pull him close.

"Maybe mine's changing, too," he said. His voice came out in puffs of air on her cheek.

They moved at the same time, and their lips met in a soft crush. Dylan used one hand to stable himself and the other to trail a thumb down her cheek.

She sighed into the kiss, wanting it to last forever. For a moment, nothing else mattered. Not the fact that they'd both just confessed to avoiding relationships, not Trent and his stupid blackmailing deal, not even the fact that despite the fact that it felt like they were the only two people in the world, alone in their boat in the middle of the beautiful glacier lake—they weren't.

"Carmen!" Her mother's voice came floating across the expanse, and echoed off the surrounding mountains. "What are you two doing back there?"

Reluctantly, Carmen pulled away. She bit her bottom lip and watched Dylan for signs of regret. "Sorry," she said. "I forgot about the parent factor."

Dylan reached out and tucked a strand of hair behind her ear. His fingers trailed down her neck, and she leaned into his touch. "Don't be sorry."

"Carmen?" her dad yelled.

Still, Carmen and Dylan didn't move. She stared into his eyes, willing him to kiss her again, because whatever objections she'd had only moments ago, she couldn't seem to remember them anymore. The only thing that mattered was the way he'd made her feel with one little kiss, the heat he'd ignited within her, a feeling she'd never felt before. Looking at him, she knew with no uncertainty that whatever it was that was happening between them, she wanted it to continue. In that moment, Carmen made the decision to phone Trent and tell him their deal was over, and she'd make that call before they left Crown Lake. She didn't want to wait any longer than she had to.

Spending the day with Carmen and her parents had been just what Dylan needed to take his mind off everything. Especially that kiss. That had been exactly what he'd needed. He hadn't kissed her again, but not because he didn't want to. Boy, had he wanted to. But knowing the relationship Carmen had with her parents and not knowing what exactly the relationship between the two of them was—he hadn't wanted to risk it.

They'd spent a few more hours paddling around and exploring the far shore. Dylan spent most of that time sneaking glances at her, and whenever he could, finding an excuse to touch her. Every time he made contact with her, even briefly, there was a spark between them, and all Dylan could think of was how badly he wanted to explore that connection between them.

He didn't look at his phone once all day. Even when Carmen excused herself to make a few calls. When the sun started to sink in the sky and Carmen announced that they should probably be heading back, he reluctantly agreed. Dylan didn't want to admit it, but he knew he couldn't play hooky forever.

Back at the Lodge, he'd said his goodbyes to Bill and Linda, who were smiling and whispering at each other, giving Dylan the distinct impression that his avoiding kissing Carmen again had all been for nothing.

"We'll see you both for dinner, then?" Bill asked. "We're just going to have a little rest and then we'll meet you at Oliver's."

"Oh, I don't—"

"Sounds great," Dylan interrupted Carmen before she could protest. "I don't know about the two of you," he continued, turning on the charm, "but all that paddling has certainly worked up an appetite."

Dylan was aware that Carmen was staring at him, but he wasn't going to let her get away so easily. Not when he had another opportunity to spend time with her.

"We'll see you soon," Linda said. Dylan knew Carmen hadn't missed the twinkle in her mom's eyes, or the little wink she gave her husband, but it didn't matter. Let her parents think they were in a relationship. Especially because Dylan himself could no longer think of many objections to making that a reality.

After Bill and Linda left, Carmen turned and stared at him. "What do you think you're doing?"

"I'm coming for dinner." He smiled smugly. "And since I

have the feeling they're already talking about us, why not give them something to really talk about?"

She tipped her head and tried to look annoyed with him, but Dylan noticed the start of a smile. "Isn't that a song?"

He reached out and tugged her into him. He'd been waiting all afternoon to hold her properly and the feel of her body against his was everything he'd expected it to be. "What's the harm?" he said, his voice husky as he moved his mouth closer to hers.

"Dylan, I don't think—"

"Then don't." He closed the gap between them and gently brushed her lips with his. Taking her soft moan as encouragement, Dylan deepened the kiss.

When he pulled back and looked into her eyes, he said, "I would like the opportunity to do that again. Wouldn't you?"

Carmen nodded but Dylan could see conflict warring in her eyes.

"Don't think," Dylan said again. "Let's just go with this."

She closed her eyes for the briefest moment before opening them and answering him with a kiss. When she broke their connection, she said, "I have a feeling I'm going to regret this. But," she bit her bottom lip before saying, "why not? Meet us for dinner at six thirty at Oliver's." She turned to walk away and shot one more look over her shoulder. "I am going to regret this, right?"

"I promise you won't."

Like a teenager, he smiled after her. He couldn't help it; something about Carmen made him happier than he'd been in a long time. And kissing her? Well, that was a different story altogether.

If he ever did decide to commit himself to a relationship, Carmen would be exactly the type of woman he'd be interested in. And for the life of him, as he watched her walk down the hall, he couldn't remember any of his objections to commitment. Carmen was gorgeous, smart, career driven—

"Where the hell have you been?"

Trent's voice came crashing through his reverie. He turned to see his big brother, storming across the lobby, fire burning in his eyes. "Trent."

"Don't you dare take that happy, easygoing, I've had a great day tone with me, little brother." Trent came to a stop in front of him and narrowed his eyes. "Where have you been? I've been calling you all afternoon."

A flash of guilt flew through him and Dylan dug his phone out of his back pocket, powering it on. Immediately, the screen lit up with missed call alerts and texts. "I had it off," Dylan said dumbly.

"Yeah. I figured that out."

"Look, I'm..." Dylan started. "What's going on?" He opted for a direct approach.

"What's going on?" Trent chuckled, but there was no humor in it. "I'll tell you. When I got your message, I tried to call you back to tell you Sam Braxton had a few more questions." Trent may as well have punched him for the nausea that immediately began to swirl in his gut as he listened.

"What do you—"

Trent held up a hand. "Just wait," he said, ice in his voice. "It gets better. When I couldn't get a hold of you, I went looking for you. I didn't find you, obviously." Trent sneered. "But what I did find was a note with your doodling on it." He held up a page from Dylan's notepad and Dylan instantly knew what Trent was going to say. To some, the note might look like a bunch of scribbles, but when you looked carefully, you could make out the dollar signs and Jake Mentz's name, and both of those things had big, scrawling Xs through them.

"Trent, it's just a doodle." Even as he protested, Dylan

knew it was pointless. The look on Trent's face told him his brother had figured out exactly what was going on.

"That's what I thought at first, too," Trent said. "And then I remembered that you tend to doodle about whatever it is you're talking about. So I phoned."

"Jake?"

Trent nodded. "And that was interesting."

Dylan knew exactly what was coming.

"Why exactly hasn't he been paid for the last few months, Dylan? Why exactly did he ask me for confirmation of funds that need to be in place before he continues work? What the hell is going on?"

Dylan shook his head. "It's all going to be okay," he said. "There was a little hiccup with financing, but with the Braxton investment, we're right on track." As he spoke, something Trent had said earlier flashed through his head. "Wait. Did you answer their questions? Did they sign?"

"They didn't."

Icy fear pricked at the back of Dylan's neck. "What? Why?"

"You weren't here," Trent continued, as if Dylan hadn't spoken. "After my chat with Jake, I knew something was up and I couldn't get a hold of you." He glared at Dylan. "And then I got a call from Sam Braxton. He said you didn't meet him for your lunch meeting, so he couldn't get his questions answered."

Dylan ran his hands through his hair, trying to control the spinning that was taking over his mind. "No," he said. "No. I totally forgot." He'd been so preoccupied with Carmen, he'd completely spaced on the most important business meeting of his career. He looked up. "Tell me he's still here."

Trent shook his head. "They left."

"No."

"I did my best to answer his questions, but they were specific to the build. And that's your—"

"Wait." A knot of ice formed in Dylan's chest. They needed that money or the Springs project would be in serious jeopardy. "We need...I need...dammit."

"They're expecting your call," Trent said. "I told them you weren't feeling well. A stomach thing. It's not over yet."

It took a second for Trent's words to register. "You what?"

"Well, I couldn't very well tell them you were off screwing around with a girl, could I?"

Anger flared in him at his brother's choice of words, but Dylan bit back a response and focused instead on the problem at hand. "I'll call them."

"Do that." Trent took a moment to straighten his suit jacket and compose himself before he added, "Fix this, Dylan. This is a partnership and if you aren't focused on the Springs project, it's not going to work."

"I'm focused."

"Are you?"

Dylan didn't miss the implication behind his words.

"I am."

Trent assessed him for a moment before nodding. "Good. Then I'll tell Carmen to back off. I can see now that it wasn't a good idea."

"Wait. What?" Dylan grabbed Trent's arm before he could leave. "What did you say about Carmen?"

He had a feeling he wasn't going to like what Trent had to say, but he needed to know.

"I'm going to tell Carmen to back off," Trent repeated. "I kind of told her to take you out so you could get your mind off of work a little bit. I see now that probably wasn't the best idea. But as your big brother, I thought you could use a little fun and—"

"Slow down." Dylan's head was spinning with everything

Trent was saying. He'd told Carmen to take him out? "What do you mean, you told her? She asked me for a drink." Dylan thought back to the other day in the lobby of the Lodge when he'd met Carmen for the first time. She'd seemed a little uncomfortable, but it had definitely been her idea to go for the drink. Hadn't it?

Trent laughed. "Carmen doesn't date, brother."

"Yeah. I got that." Dylan curled his hands into fists at his sides. "Now tell me what the hell is going on here."

Chapter Seven

WITH A SMILE ON HER FACE, Carmen put a little extra care into her clothing selection as she got ready for dinner. She didn't have a lot more than her uniform, a few sweaters, and t-shirts to choose from, but at the back of the closet she dug up a black dress she reserved for special events at the Lodge. It might be a little much for dinner with her parents, but it wasn't her mom and dad she was dressing up for.

Without a doubt, her afternoon with Dylan had been the best one she'd had in a long time, and despite trying everything to keep it from happening, in just a few short days, there was no doubt that she was developing feelings for him. Strong ones.

And more than it scared her, it confused her. Morgan was right: she had to tell Dylan about everything with his brother and their stupid deal or whatever it was. And she would, right after dinner.

She made her way to Oliver's, the upscale restaurant that was situated in the heart of the Castle Mountain Village where there were mostly a few shops and some art galleries for guests to peruse. She would have been happy eating at the Grill, but her dad insisted on treating her to an expensive dinner every time they came to visit. It was his way of showing her he loved her, and even though as far as Carmen was concerned, it was unnecessary, she played along and let him make the reservations. If it made him happy, what was the harm? Her parents were waiting for her already, but Dylan was nowhere to be seen.

Carmen paused at the hostess's stand before she made her way across the crowded room. Her mom was positively glowing, whether it be from the sun she got out on the lake, or the fun she'd had. Or maybe a combination of both; it didn't matter. But it was nice to see. Carmen smiled and watched the two of them animated in conversation.

When she approached the table, they stopped talking and her dad jumped to his feet. "Carmen? You look lovely. We were just talking about you." He kissed her on the cheek and waited for her to sit down.

"Were you?" She eyed them both suspiciously.

"Of course we were, dear," her mother said. "We were talking about how wonderful your young man is." She gave Carmen's dress a once-over. "I didn't realize we were dressing up quite so fancy." Her mom pursed her lips and tugged at the sleeves of her cardigan.

"It's really all I had clean," Carmen said. She sat down, determined not to let her mother affect her mood. "And why not dress up once in a while? I thought it would be nice."

"It is," her dad said.

"You do look nice, dear," her mother said. "But you didn't answer my question. Where's Dylan?" Her mother got straight to the point. "We had such a nice time with him this afternoon. I didn't know you had a boyfriend, dear. Really, you could have told us, you know?"

"He's not my—"

"Well, whatever he is," her dad jumped in. "He seems like

a nice young man. I for one am looking forward to getting to know him."

"Yes." Carmen looked around and glanced at her watch. "Whenever he gets here. I'm actually surprised he's not here yet. He was just going to go up and change." A knot of worry tightened in her gut, but Carmen tried to ignore it. There was no reason to be concerned about anything, she told herself. He was coming. After the kiss they'd shared, and the heat between them, there was no doubt in her mind that he'd be there. "He's probably just running late," she said. "He did have to check work messages, so maybe something came up that he had to take care of."

At the mention of business, her father perked up. "What kind of work is Dylan involved in?"

"He's building an exclusive resort in Cedar Springs. It's a community just a bit west of here and it has the most incredible hot springs that have therapeutic properties."

"Another hotel?" Her mother reached for her water and took a sip. "How nice."

Carmen resisted the urge to roll her eyes and continued talking. "It's going to be pretty amazing," she said, and she believed it. The way Dylan spoke about his project conveyed the passion and it would be pretty incredible, she had no doubt.

"It may not be anything."

Carmen swung her head around to see Dylan standing next to the table. He was still wearing his jeans and sweater that he'd been in all day, and there was a hard edge to his face that hadn't been there before.

"Sorry I'm late," he said and sat down next to Carmen. "I hope I didn't miss anything."

"No," Carmen said. She shot him a look, hoping to convey her concern at his sudden shift in mood. "I'm glad you could make it. I was just telling Mom and Dad about the Springs and how excited you are about it. What did you mean it may not be anything?"

He waved his hand, dismissing her and turned back to her parents. "There may have been a snag with some of the investors," Dylan said. He turned and looked right at Carmen, but his eyes didn't hold any of the warmth they'd held earlier and fear pricked at the back of her neck. Something was definitely going on with him. "Some new information just came to light," Dylan said.

Carmen's heart sunk. He'd been speaking to Trent. She didn't even have to ask to know the truth, but she did anyway. "Were you talking to Trent?" Her voice shook and she reached for her glass of wine to try to cover her nerves.

"As a matter of fact, I was. And it was a very interesting conversation indeed."

Carmen swallowed hard, and aware that her parents were watching them with growing interest, she asked, "Can we go and talk about it?"

Dylan shook his head and gestured around the table. "Carmen, that wouldn't be very polite. We made a commitment to have dinner with your mom and dad, and that's just what we're going to do. There'll be lots of time for talking later. Don't you think?"

She nodded, but all she really wanted to do was grab Dylan by the arm and drag him out of there so they could talk. So she could explain what really happened with Trent and his stupid blackmailing deal.

"Have you had a chance to look at the menu?"

Carmen hadn't even noticed the waitress appear next to the table. She took a deep breath and shook her head. "No. But go ahead. I don't want to hold anyone up."

While the waitress started taking orders, she absently opened her menu and stared unseeing at the choices in front of her. Hot tears pricked at her eyes, and she blinked ferociously to keep them at bay. She would not, could not cry in front of her parents. Not because of a man.

"Carmen?" Her dad's voice interrupted her thoughts and she looked up into his concerned eyes. "Do you know what you want?"

She glanced down at the menu and opened her mouth to order, but couldn't think of what to say.

"You know what?" Dylan said to the waitress. "On second thought, I think I'd like the special."

His words triggered the memory of only a few nights earlier but when she looked at him, Dylan's face didn't give anything away. He focused on her parents, and she could practically feel the chill coming off him. "I'll have the special as well," she mumbled to the waitress.

Whatever was going on with Dylan would have to wait until they were alone. For the moment, she just needed to get through dinner.

She risked another glance at Dylan, who had resumed talking to her father. Whatever Trent had said to him had upset him. That was more than obvious by his attitude, but he was there, and that counted for something. That counted for a whole lot. As did the fact that she cared so much. For Carmen, that spoke volumes.

Carmen managed to pull herself together enough to get through the evening. She kept sneaking glances at Dylan, unsure of what he was playing at. He made easy conversation with both her mother and father, and they were listening with rapt attention to every word he said. Carmen herself could barely follow the threads of what they were discussing. She did her best to pay attention, but she couldn't focus on much more than Dylan himself. Something had shifted, that was clear enough, and she knew enough to know it had something to do with what Trent may have told him. But he was there, and as uncomfortable as it was, that meant something. She just didn't know what.

By the time the dinner plates were cleared and her father leaned back in his chair, Carmen could no longer stand the tension between her and Dylan.

"How about some dessert?" her mother asked.

"I'd love to, Mom. But I actually have to work the night shift tonight to cover for the usual desk clerk. And before I go, I really wanted to show Dylan the wine cellar here."

"Oh." Her father looked disappointed, but she knew they'd understand.

"Yes," she said, and turned to Dylan. "It's really quite fantastic and maybe something you might want to replicate at the Springs. In fact," Carmen continued, unable to stand it another minute, "we should probably get going right now." She jumped up from the table and grabbed Dylan's arm.

He looked at her warily, but there was something else in his eyes, too. He knew what she was up to. Dylan stood and said, "Mr. and Mrs. Kincaid, thank you for dinner tonight. It was lovely to meet you both." He shook their hands, and Carmen quickly said a good-night to her mom and dad before dragging Dylan away.

She didn't say another word until she'd pulled him through the restaurant and into a back hallway. Carmen spun around, so she was facing him square on. "I don't know what's going on here, Dylan. But whatever Trent may have said to you, I think we need to talk about it. We can't just keep pretending that nothing is going on between us and—"

He swallowed her words with a kiss so passionate, she couldn't remember what she'd been about to say to him.

He hadn't planned on kissing her. Hell, he hadn't planned on meeting her and her family for dinner. Not after what Trent had told him. But there was a pull between them that he couldn't stay away from. And even if he was being royally played, he couldn't resist one more kiss before he did what he came to do.

When he released his hold on her, Carmen took a step backwards and caught her breath.

"Dylan, I need to—"

Dylan held a finger to her lips. "You don't need to do anything. You don't need to say anything. Trent told me all I need to know and I know I shouldn't even be here. In fact, I should be anywhere but here with you right now because every time I look at you, all I feel is anger."

"Dylan—"

"No." He shook his head. "My turn to talk. You had your chance to tell me what was going on. That you were just using me for your career. You could have told me that at any point. But you didn't."

Her face crumpled and he thought she might cry. The urge to reach out and touch her cheek, to tell her it was okay and she didn't need to be upset, was so strong that it twisted him up inside. That was the whole problem. From the minute Trent told him about Carmen and how she was using him, Dylan hadn't known what to feel.

Angry? Yes.

Hurt. Definitely yes.

She shook her head sadly. "Then why are you here, Dylan? Why did you come?"

He wanted to answer that question with another kiss. He wanted to tell her that he came because he couldn't stay away from her and despite himself, he had feelings for her. He wanted to be honest with her and open his heart the inevitable hurt that would follow.

Instead, he let the anger win. "I promised your parents I'd come," he said, keeping his face a careful mask of neutrality. "And I wanted you to know that you weren't the only one with an agenda."

"What?"

She looked up and when he looked into her deep glacier green eyes, he almost changed his mind. Dylan swallowed hard and said, "I was trying to get you to come work at the Springs." Confusion clouded her eyes. He kept his voice hard, working to control his emotions. "That's right, this whole time you were trying to get a promotion, but I was trying to butter you up to come work at the Springs when you inevitably didn't get the promotion here."

Confusion turned to hurt as she processed what he was telling her. He watched her face crumple and her beautiful eyes glisten with unshed tears and he almost took it all back and told her the truth.

"No," she said with a shake of her head.

She was right. Of course it wasn't true. Watching her fall apart, he wished he could take back every word he'd said and start over. He wanted to reach out and touch her. To bridge the gap between them. But he couldn't bring himself to swallow his pride.

"No," she said again. A tear slipped down her cheek and she swiped at it angrily. "I don't want to hear another word you have to say."

"Carmen. I didn't—"

"Leave." She spoke through clenched teeth. "You think you can come in here and interrupt my family dinner to hurt me. And you have the nerve to judge *me* for my poor choices. Who do you think you are?"

"I was angry. I'm—"

"You know what you don't know?" she asked as she paced the small hallway. "You don't know that I'd already told Trent that his whole stupid offer—that I didn't even want to be part of in the first place—was off. Did he tell you that part? Did he tell you that I didn't want anything to do with it?"

He shook his head because of course, Trent hadn't mentioned those details.

She wiped at her face again. "I told your brother that it didn't matter what the job was, or if he could help me get it. I didn't care, because what I did care about was you."

He took a step back as if he'd been slapped.

"That's right," she continued. "I care about you. Or at least I thought I did." She shook her head as if she couldn't believe it herself. "I actually thought I might be falling in love with you. I'm such an idiot."

"No, Carmen. You're not." He reached for her arm and pulled her in to him but she wouldn't look at him. "You're not an idiot."

She shook him off her and slipped away. "I am. And if you'll excuse me, I have to go. I have to work. At least, that is if I still have a job."

He watched her go, unable to find the words to bring her back. Uncertain if there were any at all.

He knew he should've have stayed away. He should have just cut his losses and never looked back.

Dylan watched her walk away from him. He stood frozen for a few minutes before leaving the restaurant out the back door. Frustrated, he pushed his way outside into the cool night air and walked as quickly as he could down the first path he saw. He didn't know where he was going. It didn't matter. He needed air. Never in his life had he felt the way he felt about Carmen, and now whatever she may or may not have done, he'd just made it that much worse.

Dylan kicked a rock on the path and yelled, letting his anger out into the night. "Dammit." He smacked his hand against a tree, the rough bark scraping his skin and it felt good to feel the pain. To feel something.

He needed to talk to Carmen, and figure out exactly what the hell was going on. They couldn't leave it the way it was. He turned back towards the Lodge, but stopped himself before he took a step towards her. No. He couldn't cause a scene while she was working. She'd never forgive that.

A confusing combination of hurt and anger flowed through him, making him restless. He paced back and forth, needing something. His skin itched with the need to know what really happened with her. He wanted to trust her; he needed to trust that she told Trent their deal was off. But he needed to know for sure.

Making a split-second decision, Dylan took a chance and turned down a side trail. Moments later, he broke into a run and pushed harder and faster until he was taking the stairs to Trent's staff housing apartment two at a time and banging on his door.

"What the hell?" Trent said as he opened the door and saw Dylan.

Dylan pushed his way past his brother into the shabby apartment. He stormed into the living room and turned around waiting for Trent to catch up.

"What the hell, Dylan?" He rubbed a hand over his face. "I was just about to—"

Unable to stand still, Dylan paced in the small room. "Tell me the truth," he demanded.

"About what?"

Dylan stopped in front of Trent, and stared into his eyes. "About Carmen. Tell me the truth."

Trent blinked and looked away. "I told you," he said. "I

asked her to go out with you as a favor to me. I know I shouldn't have, but you needed a little fun and—"

"I got that. Tell me the rest."

Trent stepped back and moved away. "There's nothing else to tell," he said with his back to Dylan.

"No?"

Trent froze.

"She didn't call you to tell you the deal was off?"

Trent didn't move.

"Trent?" Dylan moved so he was standing right behind his brother, who still hadn't answered him. "Did she call? Did she tell you that your ridiculous, blackmailing deal was off?"

Dylan held his breath, forcing himself to calm down and give Trent the chance to answer. He needed his brother to confirm Carmen's story. He had to hear it, or he didn't know what he'd do. When Trent finally shook his head slowly, the disappointment threatened to crash through Dylan.

Trent turned and said, "First of all, it wasn't blackmail." He held up a hand when Dylan tried to cut him off. "I don't know why this matters so much, Dyl," Trent continued. "You said yourself, you don't do relationships. And she's just a girl. I mean, does it really matter if she called or not? And yes, you're right, I shouldn't even have suggested it. It was a crappy thing to do. But, the fact is, she agreed to it in the first place, right? That should be all you need to know about her and how she feels about you."

Before Dylan could stop himself or even think about what he was doing, he swung and his fist made direct contact with his big brother's nose.

Trent reeled from the blow and staggered backwards into the wall, where he fell to the ground. "What the hell, Dylan?"

"The fact that there was a deal at all says a lot more about you than it does her." Dylan clenched his fists and walked towards him until he was towering over his brother, who was holding his nose, trying to stanch the flow of blood. "Now, tell me the truth, Trent. Did she call?"

"It doesn't matter."

"It does," Dylan roared.

"Yes." Trent wiped his hand under his nose, smearing blood. "She called. She told me she didn't care if she got the job or not because she didn't feel comfortable with the whole thing."

"Why?"

"I didn't ask," Trent snapped. "I was a little busy myself trying to save the Springs, remember?"

A flash of guilt for the way he'd behaved both with the Springs and with his brother hit him and Dylan offered Trent his hand. He pulled him up and handed him a washcloth to wipe his face, but he didn't apologize.

Trent took a moment to clean his face before he turned back to Dylan and said, "You don't need this, Dyl. Women are nothing but trouble. Remember what Dad used to say?"

Dylan shook his head.

"It's true," Trent continued. "Look at the last few days. You totally blew off a meeting, you put our whole project at risk, and you just broke my nose."

"I didn't break—"

"And for what?" Trent continued, ignoring him. "This isn't a good time to get messed up with a woman, Dyl. Everything's on the line and I need your complete attention on the Springs. It was a bad idea for me even to ask her to go out with you. I know that. But I just wanted you to have a little fun. I didn't think it would go this far."

Dylan walked over to the balcony and stared out at the night. He could make out the shadows of the pine trees, but not much more. Trent's question resonated through his head. Why had he done all that? What was it about Carmen that had gotten to him and made him risk everything?

"Look. I'm sorry I didn't tell you she called," Trent said behind him. His voice had lost some of its edge. "I didn't mention it because there was no point. We need to focus right now, and I never thought a few dates would lead to such a distraction. I needed you to understand that whatever you think you had with her, it wasn't real. It's not worth it, Dyl. None of this is worth it."

But it was. Dylan turned and stared at his brother. "Yes it is," he said.

"No, brother. It's not."

The Springs development was the culmination of everything they'd both worked for. He'd given years of his life to the project. If he lost it now, he'd lose everything. But there was Carmen, and if he walked away without even trying to win her, there was no doubt in his mind that he'd regret it forever.

"It's worth it," Dylan said, "because I love her."

The silence that hung in the air between them was deafening and his words echoed in his head, resonating even as they replayed. He did love her. That was exactly what he was feeling; he was just too damn stupid to recognize it before now.

"I'm sorry, what?"

"I love her," Dylan repeated.

"Harrison men don't do relationships," Trent said. "Remember?"

Dylan shook his head and laughed. "I've never felt like this about a woman before. I can't get her out of my head, Trent. I can't function. I can't concentrate on work. I just want to be with her. It's killing me. I can't explain it."

Trent shook his head but Dylan saw the realization cross his face. "You really do, don't you?"

"Yes," Dylan said. He couldn't help the smile that crept over his face. "I do."

Trent rubbed his face and examined his brother before he said, "You look like one of those idiots from the stupid romantic comedies they insist on showing on airplanes. I suppose you're going to go and sing her a song or shower her with rose petals or something equally as ridiculous, now."

Dylan nodded, his mind made up.

"I know I'm going to regret this," Trent said. "But if you really do love her, what the hell are you doing here still talking to me?"

Chapter Eight

WORKING WAS the best distraction Carmen could have asked for after the mess she'd made out of everything with Dylan. Being on the night shift meant she got to cover the front desk as well as handle any guest emergencies, and for the first few hours of her shift, things were pretty busy, with guests coming and going and calling down with questions, but then everything got quiet as she knew it would. The night shift was usually pretty dull, which could be nice on occasion, but when you were trying to forget about everything else going on, it was the exact opposite of what she needed.

At one o'clock, with four hours left in her shift, her imagination was running wild as she replayed the scene with Dylan for the hundredth time. He was angry, that much was clear. And he had every right to be, but he'd kissed her. Carmen touched her fingers to her lips, remembering the heat they'd shared. That was the confusing part. Why had he kissed her if he was just going to break her heart a moment later?

Unable to stand in place for much longer, Carmen left Quinn, her best night clerk, in charge and walked through the lobby, running her hand along the familiar wooden trim on the walls as she went. Usually, the rustic, warm room calmed her and soothed whatever hurt she was feeling, but at that moment, her sanctuary was doing the exact opposite. It felt like the walls were closing in on her, squeezing the air out of the room.

Needing some fresh air, she gestured to Quinn and went to the back door that led to the courtyard and pushed it open. She loved the Lodge, and the mountains and everything about Castle Mountain, but it no longer felt right. She wasn't going to get the general manager job, that much she knew. And she felt okay with that. She knew herself enough to know that had she been awarded the position, she would always have wondered if it was because she deserved it, or because she compromised all of her morals to hurt someone she'd grown to care about. Care very deeply about.

The strength of her feelings for Dylan, even after everything that had happened, surprised her. Never in her life had she felt that way about a man, particularly so quickly. But maybe that's what people meant when they spoke about love at first sight? A month ago, she would have thought those people were crazy. Heck, even a week ago. But now, everything had changed, and Carmen knew that aching in her chest was more than exhaustion. Much more.

She looked around the dark courtyard. Everything was so peaceful at the Lodge in the middle of the night. But as she let her eyes sweep around the space, nothing felt right. She knew it too well. She knew every corner, every valley, every inch of the place. It was comfortable and easy. There were no surprises. And maybe that was the problem. Taking a few more deep breaths of the cool night air, she went back inside and returned to her office.

Before she changed her mind, Carmen typed up a quick email. She knew she couldn't take the manager position, even if it was offered, just as she knew she could no longer stay in her current role as the customer service manager. She read over her resignation email again, and hit send.

As the email left her outbox, a sense of calm washed over her. For the first time in years, she had no idea what she was going to do, or where she was going to go. But she didn't feel panicked. It felt right.

"Carmen?"

She broke out of her reverie and looked up to see Quinn standing in her office door.

"There's someone here who wants to talk to you."

She nodded, although her insides were churning. She didn't know what to say to Dylan. Or if she could even say anything. "Thanks, Quinn. I'll be right out."

Carmen took a breath and smoothed her blouse before walking to the front desk. But it wasn't Dylan waiting for her. The sink of disappointment she felt was followed quickly by fear as she saw her mother wrapped in a robe and hugging herself.

"Mom?" Carmen hurried around the desk to meet her. "Are you okay?"

"Yes." Her mother nodded. "I'm fine. I just couldn't sleep. Your father gets snoring and I...well, it doesn't matter. I remember you saying you were going to be working the night shift, so I thought I might come and see if you wanted some company."

Carmen smiled, unexpectedly grateful for someone besides Quinn and her own mixed-up thoughts as company. "I'd like that," she said. "I'll grab myself a coffee. Would you like an herbal tea or something?"

"That would be nice, dear."

Carmen prepared their drinks, and with a quick word to Quinn, who smiled and nodded, she went to sit with her mom in the wing backed chairs by the fireplace.

"You're sure you're not tired, Mom?" Carmen asked as she handed over the tea.

"Not at all." Her mother sipped at the hot beverage. "But I did want to talk to you, dear. Sit."

Carmen eyed her mom, who, although it was the middle of the night, did not look tired at all. She was pretty sure that she herself looked like she could close her eyes and sleep for days. But that's what stress and emotions could do. Her mother did look worried, though. Icy fear trailed down her spine. Maybe that was why she was here in the middle of the night, and why they'd come a week earlier to visit.

"What's up, Mom? Is everything okay?"

"That's what I wanted to talk to you about." Carmen's heart stopped for a moment. For as much as her parents drove her crazy, if anything ever happened to them, she didn't know what she'd do.

She reached out and grabbed her mom's hand. Holding it in her own, she realized it had been a very long time since she'd held hands with either of her parents. Probably not since she was a child. She made a silent promise that as long as everything was okay with her parents, she'd hold their hands more often. "Tell me," Carmen said. She braced herself for the worst. Cancer. Heart troubles. Whatever it was, she could take it.

"Your father and I are worried about you," her mother said simply. "Something doesn't seem right with that young man of yours."

It took Carmen a second for her mother's words to sink in. "Wait," she said. "What?"

"Your young man. Dylan."

"He's not my—"

"I have to tell you, Carmen, how happy it made your father and me to see the two of you together today."

"Mom—"

"I don't know why you didn't tell me about Dylan earlier," her mother continued, completely oblivious of Carmen's distress. "Well, actually, I'm sure I do know why you didn't say anything." Her mom reached out and squeezed her hand. "I know we've never been easy on you when it comes to men and dating. We just want you to be happy, dear, and it would make me happier than anything else to see you settled with someone like Dylan."

Carmen pulled her hand away and picked at her cuticles. "Let's be honest, Mom. You'd just be happy to see me with any man. Married and preferably pregnant, right?" She tried, but failed to keep the edge out of her voice.

"Carmen Kincaid." Her mom used the tone that she used to reserve for Carmen when she was twelve and being incredibly rude. "That's not true at all. I would absolutely hate to see you in a situation that didn't make you happy. All we've ever wanted was to see you happy. Like we did today."

There was a shift in her mother's voice that caused Carmen to look up. She hadn't expected to see tears glistening in her mother's eyes. In fact, Carmen couldn't remember the last time she'd seen her mother cry. "Mom. About Dylan."

"I know. I know." Her mother held up her hand. "You two were having a bit of a fight or something. And that's why I'm here."

"What?" Carmen shook her head. "What do you mean?"

Her mother took another sip of her tea and took her time putting the cup down before she responded. "That's why I'm here. Your father and I noticed the connection between you two up at the lake. I mean, it was so clear that he's the one, Carmen."

Wait. The one? What was she talking about? Carmen's head spun, trying to keep up with her mother's train of thought.

"And," her mother continued, "it's normal for every couple

to have little arguments, especially when the chemistry is so strong between you. But it's important to know that those moments are temporary and you need to move past them and fight for the relationship you have."

"But, Mom…" She was going to tell her mom that there was no relationship to fight for, but something stopped her. "What do you mean, the chemistry is strong?"

Her mom giggled like a little girl and blushed. "I know I'm not a young woman any more, but I'm not blind either. I see the way you looked at him, and the way he was always touching you. Like he couldn't stand to be apart from you. That type of chemistry can't be faked. And it's very rare. Look after it."

Carmen lifted her mug to her mouth and let the hot coffee warm her insides while she let her mother's words sink in. There was a chemistry between them. Hadn't it been there from the moment they met? Maybe her mom was right? Maybe she did need to look after it.

"I know it's going to be hard," her mother was talking again, "when Dylan moves to his Springs. And your career is important to you, dear, and neither your father or I want to see you give that up; you've worked too hard. But the two of you will be able to make it work—I just know it. I can see it in the way you look at each other."

An image of Carmen's resignation email flying through cyberspace popped into her head. "I'm not going to be working here much longer, Mom. I decided I needed a change."

Her mom clapped her hands. "Oh, Carmen. You're going to go to the Springs with Dylan? That's just fabulous news. I know it will be a challenge for you to start at a new hotel, but if there's anything you've proved, it's that you're up for the challenge."

"Wait, Mom. No. That's not it—"

"Oh." Her mom stifled a yawn and stood from the large chair. "I think your news has given me the peace I need to sleep tonight."

Carmen stood as well and opened her mouth to tell her mom that she was definitely not going with Dylan, that they in fact weren't even a real couple and it was all a hoax. But she didn't. Instead, she smiled and said, "Good-night, Mom."

The women hugged and with another yawn, Carmen's mom wrapped her robe up tighter around her and shuffled off down the hall to her room.

Carmen watched her go and tried to process everything she'd just heard. Her parents just wanted to see her happy and they thought they'd seen that in Dylan.

She gathered up the mugs and carried them to the back room. She'd spent most of her adult life trying to prove her parents wrong and show them she could make it on her own. But what if all that time, they'd just wanted the best thing for her? What if that thing was Dylan?

As much as Dylan wanted to immediately go find Carmen and make everything better between them, or at the very least, see if there was anything left to salvage between them, he had enough sense to wait until morning.

He owed it to Trent to look after their project because for everything screwed up and wrong that Trent had done, he had done it all because he cared. And he had a point. Dylan needed to focus on the Springs, because without both of them giving the project their full attention, it would fail and neither of them could afford that.

But the one thing his conversation with his big brother had made clear to him was that there was room in his life for both business and love, and despite his best efforts to avoid it, he had fallen in love and he could no longer deny it. Nor did he want to.

He didn't get much sleep, but as soon as it was decent to do so, Dylan showered, dressed and made his call to Sam Braxton. Luckily, he knew the man was an early riser and liked to get an early start on the day. Sure enough, he answered on the second ring.

"Braxton."

"Mr. Braxton? It's Dylan Harrison. I'm so sorry I missed you yesterday at the Lodge. It was a nasty stomach bug," he lied. "And I didn't want to risk anyone else getting sick."

"You're feeling better today, I take it?"

"Much. Thank you, sir." Dylan rubbed a hand across his face, thankful the other man couldn't see him. "Trent said you had a few more questions for me," he said, eager to get to the point. "Let me see if I can answer those for you so we can move forward."

They spent the next twenty minutes discussing some of the finer points of the contract and the business aspect of the Springs. Overall, Sam Braxton was an astute businessman, and Dylan was impressed with his questions. But by the time he'd answered everything, Sam Braxton also seemed impressed.

"Well, Dylan," he said. "I think we have ourselves a new partnership. I'll be more than happy to sign the paperwork and get the first installment transferred into the account so we can keep the build on schedule."

Dylan almost cheered from the relief of the other man's words. "That sounds great, Mr. Braxton. I can't wait to share the news with Trent. Thank you very much."

When he hung up, Dylan knew he should probably go find Trent and tell him immediately that everything would be a go-ahead with the Springs. But, he settled for a quick text message and headed to the lobby. He had more pressing issues to deal with.

He was worried that Carmen would be off shift and already back in her apartment by the time he got there, but he'd already decided if that happened, he wouldn't hesitate to bang down her door until she agreed to speak to him. As it turned out, he didn't have to go to such measures. After a quick stop in the gift shop, he strode into the lobby, holding a large paper bag and found her leaving the office, with her jacket in her arms.

She didn't see him come up, which wasn't surprising, since she looked exhausted or maybe sad. Or more likely, a combination of the two. "Carmen?"

She turned and the look on her face when she registered that it was him standing in front of her almost broke his heart all over again. For a moment, he was afraid she was going to turn around and walk away. If she did that, he wasn't sure how he'd handle it. He'd planned for many different eventualities, but that wasn't one of them. He needed her to listen to him. He needed her to talk to him.

"Please," he said. "I know you must hate me right now, but—"

"Wait." She tipped her head and stared at him as if he'd just said the most ridiculous thing. "I must hate you? I know I'm tired," she said. "And I really haven't slept much. But, is that what you really just said?"

He nodded. "I was a jerk, Carmen." She dipped her head and he resisted the urge to reach out and lift it so he could look in her beautiful eyes. "I didn't mean what I said about trying to get you to work at the Springs." She looked up then. "I mean, I'd love it if you would, of course. But that was Trent's idea. He mentioned it and told me I should ask you." He was aware that he was rambling, but he couldn't seem to get the words out in the way he wanted. He took a deep breath and slowed down. "But that wasn't why I was spending time with you. And

I don't care whatever deal you may or may not have made with my brother."

She opened her mouth to say something, but Dylan laid a gentle finger against her lips. He stared directly into those eyes, so deep and green they would always remind him of the lake where he first kissed her. "Carmen." He spoke slowly, making sure she heard every word. "I was with you because from the moment I met you, I haven't wanted to be anywhere but right next to you. I can't explain it, and I don't care to try, but I've never met a woman like you before, and I certainly have never felt the way I feel when I'm with you and I don't care what brought us together. All I know is that I'm not going to stand by and let anything break us apart. Because I know you're scared, too. But scared or not, we both feel it and—"

Her lips on his swallowed whatever else he might have said. He slid a hand behind her head and drew her closer, needing to feel all of her against him.

Dylan was the one to finally break their contact. He pulled away, only far enough to look in her eyes, but kept both hands on her lower back, holding her firmly in place. He wasn't going to risk her getting away again. "I need to know," he said. "I need to know you feel the same way."

She tipped her head back and laughed. The sound escaping her throat was beautiful, and Dylan wanted to capture it to remember the moment forever. "If you need me to say it," she said after a moment, "I will."

He nodded and waited.

"I absolutely love your brother," she said.

Dylan almost dropped his hold on her, but the sparkle in her eyes gave him pause. He narrowed his eyes and said, "Oh really?"

"Absolutely. If it wasn't for him and his asinine deal, I never would have asked you to go out that first night," she said. "And

I never would have fallen completely, unexplainably, and totally in love with you."

His heart lifted at her words and he was about to pull her in for another kiss when she said, "Dylan, I'm so sorry. You need to know that—"

"No," he said, silencing her. "I know the truth about everything. And you're right. We owe Trent and his backwards, screwed-up ideas for bringing us together in the first place."

"Yeah," she said with a giggle. "We owe him a punch in the nose."

Dylan kissed her on the tip of her nose and laughed. "Already took care of it, darling."

Dylan would have been happy kissing and laughing all day, but it didn't take a genius to see that Carmen was falling asleep on her feet, and she needed to get some sleep. He walked her back to her apartment, and reluctant to be away from her, tucked her into bed and curled up behind her, pulling her close.

She snuggled into him, a perfect fit.

"Dylan?"

"I'm here."

"It's time to say goodbye," she mumbled. "I know you have work to do."

He shook his head even though she couldn't see him and inhaled the sweet smell of her shampoo that lingered in her hair. "I'm not letting you out of my sight," he said. "I want to spend every minute with you. Even if you're sleeping."

She shifted and turned in his arms so she was looking at him. "But what about later? I mean, you can't stay here forever. You have a resort to run and I..." She trailed off and wouldn't look at him.

Dylan tilted her chin up. "I know your career is here," he

said. "And I wouldn't dream of trying to take that away from you. And I don't know how we're going to do it, but we'll make it work. I care about you too much, not to make every effort to…"

Her lips turned up into a mischievous smile.

"What?" Dylan asked.

"I was just wondering," she said slowly. "I know you said you weren't trying to recruit me for the Springs, but maybe…I mean, if I suddenly found myself unemployed and looking for a change…would there maybe be a position for me there?"

Dylan didn't even try to hide the smile that spread across his face. The distance between them had been the one detail he couldn't work out, and he'd never dream of taking her career away from her. It was part of what made Carmen so strong and so special.

"What are you saying?" He tried to hide the hope behind his words.

She propped herself up on her elbow and looked down at him. "I resigned my position at the Lodge last night," she said. "At the time, I wasn't sure what I was going to do next. I just knew I needed a change. It's time. But now…I think working at the Springs might be just the challenge I'm looking for."

"Oh, yeah?" He couldn't help but tease her a little. "And the fact that I'm going to be there has nothing to do with your sudden change of heart?"

"I don't know," she said. "It may have factored in to the decision-making process slightly."

"Well, since you need a job—"

Carmen swatted at him playfully and dropped her head down next to his on the pillow. He couldn't have contained his smile if he'd tried. He picked up a few strands of her silky hair and let them slide between his fingers. "I don't know," he said, keeping his voice light, "but I think we might just be able to work something out. I know the owners."

I hope you enjoyed Goodbye Gifts! But before you go...there's still more love to be had! You might remember Lisa from past Castle Mountain books. She works in the Cub Club at the Lodge and she has a bit of a reputation...one she's looking to change. But when Jason, a handsome new guest at the Lodge, starts to flirt with her, it's not only her career on the line—but her heart, too. See how it plays out in Tempting Gifts.

You can read a sneak peak of their story right after this...

And if you want even more romance...click HERE for an exclusive FREE novella that isn't available anywhere else!

Tempting Gifts

Please enjoy an excerpt from Tempting Gifts, the next in the Castle Mountain Lodge Series

Lisa Gibbs wiped a smear of blue finger paint off her cheek and then, before the little girl who sat at the miniature table across from her could squirm away, used the cloth to clean most of the paint off her smiling face. She couldn't do anything about the paint that had found its way into her hair, but it would wash out. Besides, a messy child after arts and crafts was almost always a happy child. And if her parents didn't like it when they came to pick her up from the Cub Club, well, that was too bad.

"Why don't you go play, Emily?" Lisa suggested. "I'll put your painting on the rack to dry and you can take it with you when you leave."

The little girl nodded. "It's for my mommy. I love her the mostest."

Lisa felt the familiar pinch of jealousy. Which was ridiculous because she didn't even know the little girl's mother. But it didn't matter. She didn't need to know the woman to envy her.

Whoever she was, she had a beautiful little girl, and Lisa could guess she also had a husband who doted on her. The perfect family. Just like all the families who visited Castle Mountain Lodge.

Lisa watched Emily join a group of children building Lego before she cleaned up the painting supplies and returned them to the supply cupboard. She loved her job. Loved working with the children. It was their parents she had trouble with. They were all so damn perfect and happy and...the complete opposite from anything she'd ever had, or likely ever would.

The bells on the door chimed, alerting her to the arrival of a new guest. Instinctively, Lisa looked for Morgan. Her boss—and friend—was in the middle of reading a story to a small group who hung off her every word. Morgan waved at Lisa to handle the visitor and she nodded her response. Lisa grabbed the registration clipboard and turned around.

When she saw the man in front of her, tall and filling out his T-shirt with muscles that looked to be earned by many hard hours in the gym, Lisa momentarily forgot what to say. She'd certainly never seen him before. But that wasn't unusual at the Lodge. Guests were always coming and going, bringing their kids in and out of the child care center.

"Welcome to the Cub Club," she said. She gave him a bright friendly smile. "What can I help you with?" He didn't have a child with him, which was unusual. "Are you picking up your child?" She scanned the list, trying to figure out who he might be picking up. "Because I'll have to see some ID before we release them to you."

"Oh no. I'm not here to pick anyone up." She raised her eyebrows at his choice of words; he tipped his head briefly and gave her a strange look before he added, "I'm just wondering how this works here." He gestured around the room.

"Well, usually you have a child to register in the program." If he was some creeper who was just trying to figure out a way to be close to the kids, there was no way he'd be getting past her. The fact that he looked as if he could pick her up and throw her over his shoulder hardly seemed like an important detail. She forced a smile and tried to be as friendly as possible until she could figure out what he was after. "This is a club for kids, but if you're looking for something to do at the Lodge, I could direct you in the right direction. We have a wide variety of activities for our older guests as well, sir." She put her clipboard down and looked at him pointedly.

"Oh no." A smile crossed his face and he laughed as he realized what she was implying. "It's not like that at all."

Lisa's instincts were to believe him. Despite his broad chest and thick arms, he didn't look like the threatening type. In fact, he looked like the type of guy she would normally be attracted to. Very attracted. But that was before. Things were different now and a man, even one as attractive as the one who stood in front of her, was not on her agenda. "Well, how is it then, sir?"

"Jason," he said. "My name's Jason. And I actually am wondering about the Cub Club. Not for myself obviously," he added quickly.

The man crossed his arms over his chest, which drew more attention to them as far as Lisa was concerned. She tried not to stare at his defined muscles.

"Obviously." She looked directly into his big green eyes. "That would be weird."

He chuckled and nodded. "That it would. But don't worry, I'm not some kind of crazy. I actually need to register Kayden."

"Kayden? That's a nice name."

"Yeah. His mom named him after his grandfather." There was a time, not too long ago, when Lisa would've inquired further about Kayden, his mom, and whether his extremely good-looking and charismatic father was a single father and potentially in need of a date. But that was before she almost lost everything she'd worked for at the Lodge because of her tendency to flirt, and well, more than flirt, with guests. After the Gage Mitchell incident, when she took her attraction to the movie star who was staying at the Lodge a little too far, she was lucky she still had a job at all. And there was no way she was going to make that mistake again. Things had changed. She had changed.

She glanced up from her clipboard where she'd started writing. "Okay." She returned her attention to the clipboard with the professional detachment she'd perfected since the *incident*. "We can get your son registered without a problem. How many days will you be visiting us at Castle Mountain?"

She held the pen poised in her hand and waited for his response. When he didn't say anything, she looked up. "Sir? How many days?"

"It's Jason," he said finally. Amusement laced his voice. "Remember?"

"I remember." She returned his smile. He was so disarming, she couldn't help how her body responded to him. "How many days would you like to register for, Jason?" She emphasized his name this time. "Basically, how it works is every day we plan different activities for the children so they can enjoy some fun, kid time, and you and um…Kayden's mom…"She tilted her head with the implied question that she knew she had no business asking and tried to tell herself that she didn't care what the answer was. When Jason only shrugged in response, she continued. "Well, then the two of you are free to enjoy some of the activities at the Lodge that aren't quite so child friendly, and everyone has a good time."

"Sounds good," Jason said. "I'll sign him up for the day after tomorrow."

"Great. You said your son's name was Kayden?" Lisa scribbled down the date next to his name.

"Oh, he's not my son."

His words caught her and she looked up and took a deep breath. "Okay," she said. "Your stepson then?"

Jason chuckled. Apparently he found her funny. "I never said he belonged to me. Kayden's actually my nephew. My sister's still checking in so I thought I'd come down and take care of things for her."

A flush passed over Lisa's face. She really shouldn't jump to conclusions. "I'm sorry," she said. "I just assumed. But we generally only get parents coming into the Cub Club. It was an easy mistake."

"And do you flirt with all the parents?"

"I wasn't flirting." Lisa thrust her shoulders back and crossed her arms, because the last thing she was doing or intended to do was flirt.

"Oh, really?" He grinned.

She wanted to be irritated by his grin, but it only made him more attractive and that was way too dangerous. "Absolutely not." She shook her head and narrowed her eyes into a glare.

"Well," he said with an easy smile, "if you were, I'd be flattered."

Damn it. *He* flirted with *her*.

She bit her bottom lip a little and forced any and all thoughts that were even remotely inappropriate from her head. She wasn't going to go down that road again. Not even for a man who looked like Jason. She shook her head firmly. "Sorry to disappoint, but I was just doing my job. I am definitely not interested." She emphasized the words so there'd be no further misunderstanding. And by the transformation on his face, Lisa was pretty sure he got the point. A part of her, especially the part that thought he was a nice guy, felt bad.

"If you say so."

"It's not that—"

"Hey, whatever you say." He tucked his hand in his back pocket, a move so effortlessly casual, it made Lisa's stomach flip in a way that both annoyed and excited her. "So, what else do we need to get Kayden registered?"

Lisa swallowed hard; for some unknown reason, she felt the need to explain. "Look, it's not you; it's just that I kind of make it a point not to date guests." She searched his face for an indication that he wasn't still upset with her, and she couldn't help but wonder why she cared at all. He was just a guest. He'd be gone in a few days, and as long as she behaved, she'd still have her job. It wasn't like her to care about what anyone thought, let alone some random guy she'd just met. But there was something about Jason. "Seriously. If it wasn't for that, I would totally be flirting with you." *Why on earth did she just say that?* Lisa bit the end of her pen to keep from talking any more.

His eyes flashed, and the corner of his mouth turned up in a wicked grin. "And what makes you think it was a *date* I was interested in? I had something much different in mind."

He emphasized the word date and his eyes flashed with a look Lisa had become all too familiar with when it came to men. She took an automatic step back and shook her head. Anger flooded through her. Did he really just proposition her? Clearly her read on men was slipping. It was just her luck that the most gorgeous man she'd laid eyes on in months was also a complete ass.

It took her a moment to recover, and then with a renewed determination for professionalism, she picked up her clipboard and tried to resume the check-in. Anything to get Jason, and everything he suddenly represented, away from her as quickly as possible.

"What room are you in?"

"I thought you weren't interested?" His eyes were hard, but she detected an edge of amusement in his voice. "But if you insist—"

A hot blush shot across her face. "I need it for the form."

"If I knew it, I'd tell you. But I don't have it yet." His grin got wider. "Just put it under Porter."

She scribbled down the name. "And anyone who will be picking up or dropping Kayden off? I need their names. His mother, perhaps a girlfriend or—"

"My sister's name is Jennifer. I don't have a girlfriend."

Despite how obnoxious he was, the piece of information caused an annoying flutter in her chest. "Okay, and how many days are you staying with us?"

"Five days."

Five days? That was long enough to get to know him. The idea popped into her head before she could stop it. What was she even thinking? He was clearly a player and even if she hadn't sworn off men, Jason should be the last guy she'd consider. She did not need that type of drama in her life.

"Five days is a long time," she said with as much detachment as she could muster. "I'm sure you'll be able to take in a lot of what the Lodge has to offer."

"Doubtful." He rolled his eyes. "I'm here for a family reunion."

"Well, that sounds fun, too." She raised her eyebrows.

"I don't know about that." He shoved his hands in his back pockets, and in an instant, the arrogant man he'd been melted away to reveal the friendly, approachable man she'd met originally. "But it's been awhile since I've been up to the mountains. I forgot how pretty it is up here. I'm looking forward to exploring, maybe a hike or a—"

"Doesn't sound much like a reunion."

"Honestly?" Jason leaned in and whispered. "That was just an excuse to get up to the Lodge."

"Well, now that you're here," Lisa swallowed hard, a chill going down her spine at his closeness, "I hope you find what you're looking for."

He was so close his scent filled her senses. It was a spicy, manly scent, almost like cinnamon, but richer. Almost like chocolate. She fought the urge to pull away even though it was exactly what she should be doing. What was it about this man? She should have been running in the opposite direction, yet something about him drew her in at the very same time it pushed her away. Confusion roiled through her.

"I'm sure I'll find exactly what I'm looking for," he said after a moment.

His words were loaded with expectation and innuendo. But despite the draw, she had to stay strong and stick to her rules. Especially with a man who so obviously was only in it for the short term. It was probably part of his game to find a holiday fling and she was definitely not in the mood to be anyone's game. No thank you.

Lisa was just about to step back and put a safe distance between them when she heard a voice behind her.

"Lisa?"

She froze and then spun around to see Morgan stood behind her, a frown on her face.

"Is everything okay here?" Morgan asked.

"Of course, I—"

"He was just—"

Morgan looked at both of them in turn. Her eyes narrowed. Eventually she turned to Lisa. "Why don't you take a break?"

Lisa looked back at Jason before she turned to Morgan again. She did not look impressed and no doubt she thought Lisa was hitting on the guests again despite all of Lisa's promises to the contrary. She flicked a look at Jason. Damn him. It was all his fault. He'd done this and he was probably going to go away and have a good laugh with his buddies or his family or whatever, at her expense. She narrowed her eyes and opened her mouth to protest again, but there was no point.

Morgan was going to be pissed. That was for sure. Without bothering to look at Jason again, she nodded and walked away.

There was no doubt that Morgan would want to talk about it as soon as she was done with Jason, but she might as well save her breath. Lisa wasn't a fool: despite all of her best efforts since the Gage Mitchell incident, her reputation was a hard one to shake. It's not as if she meant to go over the line—it just happened. Things probably would have been different if her attraction with Gage Mitchell had panned out exactly how she'd planned. But that definitely hadn't worked out, and looking back, it was probably for the best.

No, it was definitely for the best. Lisa smoothed her hair back into a ponytail, and tried to rid herself of the memory. She'd decided then that she really needed to stop acting so loose with men. And she had, too. She spared a quick glance to where Morgan still talked to Jason. For the most part.

"Lisa?" A little voice provided her with the distraction she needed. She looked down at the little girl she'd been painting with earlier.

Lisa crouched so she was at eye level. "What's up, kiddo? Do you need something?"

"Will you play with me? I wanna build blocks, but they keep falling."

Lisa smiled and tucked a strand of Emily's hair behind her ear. "I would love to." She took the little girl by the hand and let her lead the way to the corner where the blocks were kept.

Something caused her to glance in Jason's direction one more time as she handed Emily the first block. He took a piece of paper from Morgan, likely his reminder slip, and turned to leave. But before he did, he looked in her direction and their eyes locked. He opened his mouth as if he wanted to say something, but Lisa shook her head and focused on Emily. Kids were easier.

The second he was out of the Kids Club, Cub Corner or whatever it was called, Jason Porter slammed his hand against the wall and cursed. Seconds later, he looked around to make sure no one had seen him. It was a bad habit, gleaned from too many months up North working in the oil patch, but he knew his twin sister, Jennifer, would rip up one side and down the other if she heard him swear like that.

But sometimes there were no other appropriate words for a situation. Like the way he'd just royally screwed things up with the prettiest girl he'd seen in months. And it wasn't just that she was pretty, although with her blond hair, and womanly curves that just begged for him to—no. He wasn't going to go there. It didn't matter anyway, after the way he'd just behaved. He'd more or less offered her a one-night stand. Regardless whether that was the only type of relationship he cared to have these days, it hadn't been appropriate. And he'd offended her. Any idiot could see that.

But why did it bother him so much? He'd never let it affect him before.

He knew why. Even if he didn't want to admit it. The truth was, Lisa was the first woman he'd been even remotely interested in since Nikki, and that was a long time ago. Not that it mattered, because she wasn't likely to even speak to him again, never mind go out with him. Which was probably a good thing, because dating wasn't an option for him. Not anymore.

He wasn't interested. Not really. At least that's what he could—and probably should—keep telling himself. A date wasn't going to happen, not even if it was just a super casual drink at a hotel where he'd never see the woman again. No. Especially not that. Maybe in a different time, or a different…it didn't matter.

There was no point giving the situation anymore time and

energy. Not when he could be out enjoying the mountains or the Lodge itself, which might as well have been the royal palace compared to the basic camps he was used to up North. And he should definitely be enjoying his little nephew, Kayden. It was after all, the only reason he'd agreed to his sister's incessant nagging to go to the stupid family reunion. The last thing he really wanted was to have to make small talk with cousins he hadn't seen since…well, it had been awhile, and he certainly hadn't missed any of them. There was a reason it'd been so long.

But he was here, and he'd play nice, mostly because it would make Jennifer happy and after all, that's what he did. Made his sister happy. He made his way down the corridor to the lobby, where she was hopefully done checking them in. He'd offered to look into the kids club thing for Kayden, mostly to get away from the crush of people, most of whom were relatives who all clambered for a position at the front desk. Details really weren't his thing. He'd let Jen take care of that.

"Hey, buddy." Jason ruffled Kayden's hair and plopped down next to him on one of the plush leather couches in the main reception area. "Where's your mom?"

Kayden pointed to the desk. "She told me to wait here."

"Probably for the best. This is the worst part of staying in a hotel." His nephew nodded his head in agreement. "But do you know what the best part is?"

They looked at each other and said in unison, "The pool!"

"Can we go, Uncle Jason?"

"Of course." He glanced toward his sister who finally, mercifully, made her way toward them. "But let's wait and get settled in our rooms, okay?"

"What are you waiting to do?" Jennifer raised her eyebrow in question. "I'm sure it has something to do with the schedule of events, right?" She smiled and Jason didn't even bother to stifle his groan.

With their dark hair and green eyes, there was no doubt they were siblings, but that's where the similarities ended. Where Jason was always quiet, and preferred to hang out with a few close friends or spend his free time outside, Jennifer had always been the more wild, impulsive twin. She thrived on large groups of people, parties and being the center of attention. A trait that had meant Jason spent most of their high school years playing the role of the protective big brother, making sure the boys who were clamoring for his beautiful sister's attention were worthy. They often weren't. And unfortunately, Jason hadn't been able to prevent his sister from choosing the wrong man to marry and ultimately divorce.

Although, the one good thing that came from that union was his nephew. And that was a pretty damn good thing. Plus, now that she was a mother, Jennifer had completely changed, except when it came to wanting be around lots of people. Hence, the reunion.

"Come on, Jason." She shoved an envelope at him. "That's why we're here."

"What's this?" He eyed the envelope somewhat suspiciously but didn't open it.

"Your itinerary for the weekend."

With one last look at the envelope, Jason stood and shoved it in his back pocket. "Right." He grabbed the bags. "Why don't we go find our rooms?"

Kayden leapt up and led the way across the large timber framed lobby to the bank of elevators. Jason smiled and gathered up the bags. As they made their way across the room, Jason was careful not to make eye contact with any of his cousins. He knew he couldn't avoid talking to them forever, but he did plan to put it off for as long as possible. Instead he focused on the large picture windows that covered the entire back wall of the lobby, and the magnificent view they afforded. It had been a long time since he'd been in the mountains, too long, and he couldn't wait to get out there.

"You know you're going to have to hang out with them a little bit." Jennifer read his mind, the way she always did, but Jason only shrugged and shook his head.

"Not if I can help it."

"Jason." She turned to look at him as they waited for the elevator. "That's why you're here. It's a family reunion."

"No." He stabbed his finger at the button again. "That's why you're here. I'm here to be with you. And Kayden." He smiled at his nephew. "And that's exactly what I plan on doing. And you know, I checked out that kids club thing." The face of the beautiful blond, with her fiery eyes glaring at him, flashed through his mind. "But I don't know if that's the right thing for Kayden."

"Why not? The lady at the desk said they did lots of fun things, like crafts and hikes and even scavenger hunts."

"Scavenger hunts?" Kayden was always listening, and had twigged onto the one thing that he'd liked the sound of. "I wanna do that."

"I'm sure we can sign you up—"

"I don't think it's—"

Kayden looked between them and shook his head. He was used to his mom and his uncle disagreeing. He also knew his mom made the final decision.

"We'll sign you up." She shot Jason a look.

"He already is," Jason mumbled and thankfully, the elevator arrived and without another word, he picked up the bags. "The day after tomorrow." There was no point arguing with his sister. She'd win. She always did. Besides, Jennifer was right: Kayden would have fun in the kids group, and there weren't very many little cousins his age. The whole family reunion would be even more excruciatingly boring for his nephew than it would be for him.

And more than boring, and dealing with his extended family, it would be the constant reminder of what Jason had once, and had lost.

Their rooms were next to each other, down a long hall, and after Jason dropped the bags in Jennifer and Kayden's room, he looked forward to a bit of time alone. Of course, his sister had other plans. Before he even had time to cross the room and open the curtains, there was a knock on the door that attached their two rooms. He could ignore it. Pretend he hadn't heard it. But that would only buy him a few minutes. When his sister wanted something, there was no way she gave up.

With a flick, he unlatched the deadbolt and seconds later, the door opened, and his sister stepped inside. "Kayden's jumping on the beds, trying to decide which one he wants to sleep in, so I thought I'd come and see how you're doing."

"Why wouldn't I be doing okay?" Jason tugged the cord that opened the thick curtains and let the sunlight spill into the room. It was a beautiful fall day, and although he knew the weather could change in an instant up in the mountains, for the moment it was beautiful.

"Come on, Jason. I know you. I know this can't be easy."

Without turning away from the view, he said, "What? Being around all these people who share our name, but not our lives? Who pretend to care about us, but really just want a good story to talk about around their dinner table at Sunday night dinner? You think that's hard? I don't understand."

"That's not fair." He turned to see his twin, with her arms crossed over her chest. "You know that's not fair. They're not all like that."

"But most are."

Jennifer started to shake her head in protest, but turned it into a shrug instead. "Okay, I admit, our family wasn't totally supportive after…well, when Nikki died, I know they weren't the best." The mention of her name prompted the familiar pain in his chest, although admittedly, it wasn't as sharp as it had been.

"No, Jen. Our *family*. Mom, Dad, you and Kayden. You guys were great. Everyone else, well they can go to—"

"Uncle Jason!" Kayden's head appeared in the doorway, promoting a warning look from Jennifer. Not that he needed it —Jason would never swear in front of his nephew. Not intentionally anyway. "Isn't it cool? Our rooms are totally attached."

Jason grinned. How could he not? His real family was right here in the room with him. With the exception of his parents, who had to take a last-minute business trip instead of joining them. It was probably for the best anyway, considering his dad mostly shared Jason's feelings regarding his own family, despite the fact that most of them worked for the family business, Porter Properties. Jason had somehow managed to avoid taking a position there, despite his father's constant asking. Nikki's death had changed a lot of things. Too many.

Maybe his stay at the Lodge won't be as bad as Jason thought? But will his flirting cost Lisa her job?
Read the rest of Tempting Gifts now!

About the Author

Elena Aitken is a USA Today Bestselling Author of more than forty romance and women's fiction novels. The mother of 'grown up' twins, Elena now lives with her very own mountain man in the heart of the very mountains she writes about. She can often be found with her toes in the lake and a glass of wine in her hand, dreaming up her next book and working on her own happily ever after.

To learn more about Elena:
www.elenaaitken.com
elena@elenaaitken.com